Swamp Magic

Bobbi Romans

*To Amanda
Thanks for Coming!
Hope You Enjoy.
Bobbi Romans*

CRIMSON ROMANCE
F+W Media, Inc.

Published by
Crimson Romance
an imprint of F+W Media, Inc.
10151 Carver Road, Suite 200
Blue Ash, Ohio 45242

www.crimsonromance.com

Copyright © 2012 by Bobbi Romans

ISBN 10: 1-4405-6425-6
ISBN 13: 978-1-4405-6425-3
eISBN 10: 1-4405-6426-4
eISBN 13: 978-1-4405-6426-0

This is a work of fiction. Names, characters, corporations, institutions, organizations, events, or locales in this novel are either the product of the author's imagination or, if real, used fictitiously. The resemblance of any character to actual persons (living or dead) is entirely coincidental.

Dedication

To my Belle's—T, Nikki, Char, Hula and Boo—thanks for always lending an ear for late night ideas.
To Linda—Ditto. :)
Most of all…
To my real life Prince Charming and family who, when others laughed, believed and pushed.

Chapter One

The swamp air sat heavy on her skin, as her water-soaked feet sank deep within the bog's smelly muck. With each mud-laden step, Beth was certain she would lose one, if not both, of the fugly combat boots her brother had insisted she wear. She'd cursed him at the time, but was now more than grateful to have on the snake-proof boots. Whenever she found Robby's ass and they got out of this godforsaken place, she'd kill him. No, scratch that. Skin him, then kill him.

Damn, but she should have listened to Kara and kept her butt at home rather than gone out traipsing through this mosquito-infested, hot as Hades swamp, trying to track down some elusive-ass bog monster. She'd ignored her best friend, listening instead to her whacked-out brother while her inner Nancy Drew leapt at the prospect of a mystery. Now she was wandering lost, in the swamp…at sunset, no less. She'd rather be at home getting ready for bed, and hopefully another night with her dream man. Her faceless hero, whom though she'd never seen, knew would play some important part in her life.

But no, color me stupid. She'd let her brother talk her into it. She was hot and miserable as she slapped at yet another mosquito while silently cursing herself.

Irritable, she plucked at her sweat-soaked tee. She didn't think she'd ever been so stanky in her whole life. A quick sniff to her pits served as confirmation. Good grief, surely the bog monster would hightail it in the opposite direction at the first ungodly whiff of her. So would any other living thing, she prayed, since darkness had fallen, and the night creatures had come out to play.

An owl hooted right when she began to step over a log and right as something tapped her thigh. Her scream hit octaves she hadn't known she possessed as some fast-paced high kicking had her precariously perched atop the next closest log.

Shaking, it took her a few minutes of squinting through the darkness with only the aid of her fading flashlight before she realized her attacker was just a limb floating by. Whew. She'd feared a gator, or, worse, a slithery snake or lizard.

Beth glanced about, if not for being lost, she'd almost be relieved no one was around to see her right now. Right, like who the hell would see? She was in the middle of freaking nowhere and worried about someone seeing her acting like a big weenie and not the capable self-sufficient woman she was.

Shaking her head, she sat and tried to gather her bearings. Reaching behind her, she grabbed a wad of humid frizzy hair and attempted to plait the jet-black mess enough she'd be able to tuck the end inside the plait itself. The loose tendrils stuck to her back and face, driving her batshit crazy.

Okay, now think, Beth, think. You last saw Robby and his doofus buddies by the old shack. You then, like a dumb ass, went searching for them heading east…so said shack should be around the bend, a little more west.

Certain of her whereabouts, she cautiously stepped off the log, noting the thick, lily-pad-covered water swirling to her right and said a quick prayer that whatever caused the swirl wasn't deadly. The last snake she'd seen had her climbing a cypress tree faster than most of the raccoons she'd passed.

Maybe if she moved really fast? No, predators were attracted by quick movements. Fast might not be the best idea. Almost hypnotically, her gaze drew back to the swirling, as the water almost seemed to turn iridescent. She shone her flashlight more toward the center, whacking the dying metal thing on her palm a few times to no avail. Relief washed over her when she saw no evidence of red glowing eyes lurking nearby. The glow, a sure telltale sign of gators lying in wait.

Shit, why the hell hadn't she paid more attention to those damn survival shows her brother always made her endure? What was the one show, *Man Against Wild?* Well, how about *City Brat Against Wild?* Wild would win, without a doubt.

She scanned the area again and prayed she had indeed headed in the right direction. If not, she faced a long, tedious, and frightening night.

Well, she sure as hell wasn't getting to the cabin perched up on the damn stump. She wanted out of this godforsaken swamp with the humidity from hell. Not to mention getting away from the prehistoric-sized bugs swarming all around.

The water eerily stilled as the swamp sounds came to an abrupt halt. No screeching hoot owls, no more insanely loud chirps from crickets. *Nothing.* No movement or sound pierced the night. Complete and utter silence greeted her. The loss of the natural sounds terrified her more than anything else. Something had spooked the critters and bugs, and her gut screamed that whatever it was, with her luck, was so *not* a good something.

Time to go. She slid off the log and began wading toward the cabin—or, rather, she *hoped* toward the cabin.

She felt more than heard the water swirling about her calves and whipped around to search for its source. Her heart rate went into overdrive, as her palms grew sweaty, making it harder and harder to retain her death grip on the flashlight.

Turning, she began taking cautious steps backwards toward the bend and the hopeful safety of the shanty she'd seen. Her beam was now dim; the heavy-gauge metal was more weapon than light as she raised it over her head, aiming toward the swirls moving the deeper water to her right. In the midst of the strange whirlpools, the odd yet mesmerizing iridescence came back. Only this time it wasn't *almost* glowing—it *was* glowing. The eerie, greenish blue spiraled about madly, only visible here and there as it peeked out between the many lily pads, obscuring her view.

Swamp Magic

Terror gripped her, anchoring her in place as headlights do a deer over the freaky happenings before her. Trembling, her mind screamed to turn and run, but her body refused to heed her mind's clear warning. Her heart beat with such velocity she swore it would burst from her chest at any moment. She couldn't even seem to will breath into her body, and her lungs grew heavy. Her breathing became no more than ragged gasps as she began to hyperventilate.

Her eyes widened as the active water began to become more centered. Fear froze her immobile. Though terrified, she continued to be drawn, almost as if in a trance, into its strange murky depths. Her vision zeroed on the brightest point amid the swirls, jaw gaping open as a form began to emerge.

The form of a man.

He rose from the murky depths like some type of Greek deity, Neptune perhaps. Her mouth grew dry as he continued his slow rise, inch by glorious inch. Terror receded as blatant curiosity arose. She tried to lick her parched lips as droplets of water ran down his wet, chiseled chest and continued running until they disappeared into the low-slung waistband of his pants. Pants which, luckily for her, were good and wet and plastered to his magnificent body, leaving little to the rest of her imagination. She nibbled her bottom lip, wanting to lick just one of those lucky, lush little droplets rolling down him.

One jerk of his head moved the long, dirty-blond hair enough to reveal the face of a god. Eyes so intensely green she swore they penetrated her soul. And shoulders, oh, so big, they would devour her if she were embraced within. Bronzed skin that had been kissed by many a sunray, abs that rippled right down his belly. Part of a beautiful tattoo was visible as it spread about his stomach in a unique pattern, seeming to come from his back.

She'd gone mad. She should be running in stark fear, yet here she stood watching a man emerge from the swamp and wondering about being wrapped safely in those huge arms. Her fingers itched to run them over every hard, muscled ridge, all the way down to...

Too much heat—yes, that explained everything. She'd passed out from heat stroke and this was some weird delusion. *One smoking hot sex delusion at that.* It had been quite a while since she'd been with anyone intimately.

Her vivid delusion began heading straight toward her, a severe look drawn on his face, almost hungry and predatory in nature.

Holy smokes, she thought, licking her lips at the sight. Again her eyes drew toward what lay just below those fabulous abs as hip bones sculpted the most perfect V shape she'd ever seen. Her imaginary man would have been better completely and utterly naked; however, her luck seemed to have run out in that department.

The delusion seemed to beckon her as it stretched out a hand and one long finger pointed at her and began motioning her toward him. All the iridescent colors coming from him and the water began blending with the night and foggy air, swirling faster and faster in a tornadic display of light and color. Her head swam with it all, until from the heat, shock and fear, she succumbed to the pull of oblivion, and sank welcomingly into it.

Beth Sloan awoke slowly and very groggily to her head bobbing and the knowledge she was upside down. The water seemed much too far away now for her current liking. She threw out a hand to brace herself enough to sit up, and when it contacted warm, hard, living flesh, her eyes flew open at once.

Chapter Two

With no other choice, she gripped the rather large biceps her hands braced against and hauled herself into a partially lifted position to better view who the hell's back she rode on. Her mind flittered to the hunky hallucination from earlier.

"Oh, shit." The feel of warm, hard male flesh slid beneath her palms as a musky, masculine scent flooded her senses, which meant one thing. Her delusion was real.

"Who…who are you?" she stuttered, craning her neck to discover an incredibly sexy backside. She glanced downward again, and had to admit, her former delusion owned a fantastic ass as well. Now, if she only knew who the owner of said ass was.

As if he'd read her thoughts, his steps faltered and he paused to set her before him. He turned a dark, dangerous gaze in her direction, and she fought the reflex to run knowing it wouldn't do her any good anyway.

God, she'd never seen eyes quite that shade of green before. Almost swamp green, similar to jade, only much deeper, if such a thing were possible. And those lips. She just wanted to nibble her way up to them. Good grief, but another round of carnal lust surged at a mere glance from the smoking hot hulk of a man carting her off to where? Never Never Land? Maybe she was mentally surfing some Tarzan-type fantasy she hadn't realized she'd harbored.

The intensity of her body's response to this stranger perplexed her even more. "You may call me Moss," his rich voice declared. Each timbered syllable seemed to vibrate clear through her. Of course, being held in his arms like this had many naughty thoughts running amok through her. Thoughts of being pinned against a wall as he took her hard and fast while she locked her thighs around his slim hips for the wild ride. Of being taken, owned and worshipped.

She gazed again into the green depths of his eyes and caught something flickering just below the surface. A hunger that seemed to lie dormant within, and she sensed a surreal loneliness almost rolling in waves from him. More than mere sexual arousal, he aroused her body and soul. Her heart reacted to him as did her nipples, which had grown firm and tender.

Screw whether any of it made any sense. All she cared about was finding that damn cabin and getting rid of all her sexual frustrations. She had no doubt this swamp man could fix all that ailed her.

*

Moss scented her sudden flare of desire. He fought to keep his beast at bay. It had been so long since he'd released his need with a woman rather than by his own hand. He wanted this one as much as she wanted him. With her ebony hair, olive skin, and breasts peaked in perfection, he knew beyond doubt she was as needy. Her arousal was quite apparent through the alluring thin white tee she wore and heady scent perfuming from her. He wondered if she realized how transparent her shirt had become in the swamp's humid air. He could make out every unique detail of her breasts, from the color of her areolas to the slightly different shade of her puckered nipples. Between the visual feast and her erotic scent, the little female was driving him insane. White had just become his favorite color for a woman…white and wet.

He had to move slowly, as the last thing he wanted to do was frighten her more than she already was considering she'd passed out. Who the hell brought a woman out into the dangerous Florida swamps—at night, no less? No normal human dared venture out into the gator-infested waters, much less alone. Her mate should be shot for allowing her out like this. When he found the cad, he'd teach him a lesson in the proper care of a woman. *His loss, my gain,* Moss wickedly thought as images of the female naked and beneath him raced to the forefront of his mind. His at least for the moment, and he planned to take full advantage of every second with this wanton little creature.

"Oomph."

He ignored her startled gasp when he hoisted her over his shoulder again, and simply said gators when she attempted to protest being hauled around. That one word, gator, stilled her into compliancy.

Moving with more speed than necessary, he rounded the corner and watched as recognition flittered over her expression at the cabin looming ahead. He'd sensed her fear dissipate and though he'd have been content to stand there for hours appreciating her beauty, especially the bashful yet heated looks she sent his way, her human status made her vulnerable to sickness. He didn't know when her worthless mate might come looking for her, if the louse wasn't doing so already. Best get her inside and warmed up. He hoped in more ways than one.

Kneeing the door open, he entered and laid her gently down on the old antique bed. Her expression was intense and curious as she studied him, biting on her lower lip as if trying to decide something. Though he didn't doubt under normal circumstances they would have shared a connection, he couldn't help but wonder how much of the lust he sensed from her came from the pheromones his kind produced.

"Oh, fuck it. I've never been this impetuous before, but… but…" she whispered as her cold hands shot to each side of his face, and pulled his lips to hers. Explorative, curious, and hungry, her wet tongue swept past his before sucking on his bottom lip. As much as he wanted to pursue the intensity of her kiss, he wanted her warm and void of any possible future illness. The swamp might be as hot and humid as Hades during day hours, but at night a chill rode the air. Mortals tended to be so susceptible to swamp-borne illnesses.

He grabbed her hands and held them for a moment before breaking the kiss.

"Wait." He'd meant his voice to come out soft but instead it grated out husky…gruff. His own need became overbearing as his erection turned downright painful.

Somehow, that lone word penetrated what he assumed was a momentary, lust-filled lapse in her judgment. He watched her visibly go from lusty to wary in nary a second as she seemed to play tug of war with herself. He saw her body's response to his, yet her mind, being more practical, warned her away.

Which would she listen to, he wondered anxiously, her body or her mind?

"What is it with you?" she finally asked. "Why do I find you so utterly compelling? Familiar even."

"Compelling? I do not recall anyone ever describing me as such." He wasn't sure what she meant. Had she complimented him, or referred to him as strange?

Beth cringed as the implication of her previous actions sank deep. Good grief, she'd acted like some kind of bitch in heat. If he hadn't stopped her, she would have continued, without any hesitation whatsoever. *None.*

No, she could control herself. Yes, control was a good thing. Sitting up and straightening her back, she slid to the edge of the bed, setting her resolve to firm. Sitting so rigidly strained her breasts against her tee and made her all the more aware of just how wet she'd become. She'd give her right arm for some warm dry clothes right now.

Beth watched as he turned abruptly away and began attending to the small hearth. She hoped he was going to start a fire, as the cabin had grown chilly without the heat he'd stirred within her.

Chilled?

She glanced down. Sure as shit, her nipples jutted against the wet tee in complete, look-at-us-here-we-are fashion. Mortified, she crossed her arms over the frozen peaks.

Chapter Three

Beth caught the heated look and odd flare of his nostrils just before he'd turned away. She realized he hadn't missed what she'd just become aware of and subconsciously drew her arms tighter together. Heat bloomed in her cheeks over how oblivious she'd been about her wet tee.

She observed him in quiet admiration as his attentions remained fixed to the ancient-looking fireplace he fiddled with. Beth took in the fine view his backside offered. She bet a coin would bounce right off that derriere of his. No matter how hard she tried, her wild mind veered back to decadently erotic thoughts.

Once the fire cackled to life and its ember flames danced among the dry wood, he rose and headed toward a small chair off in the corner. When he rose to his full height, the cabin appeared to shrink around his massive muscular body. He appeared completely unabashed by his nudity as he stripped off his wet pants, showing no hesitation or embarrassment at the fact he now stood nude, nor that his boner bobbed up against his belly. Hell, he seemed to be sporting the thing like a badge of honor. Yet there she sat, crossing her arms to cover the outline of her tits and fighting to keep her hormones in check.

She would put him at around six foot four, maybe 240 pounds. Yeppers, 240 pounds of pure, aroused beefcake. She should say something, but words congealed in her throat even as decadent thoughts flashed through her mind.

Her hand shot to her mouth, checking to see if drool had formed in the corners. A glance at his expression confirmed the cocky look he wore, and again she worried he could read her mind. If he could...

She trembled, and it had jack to do with the chill and more to do with the slow steps of the man approaching her. She would almost describe it as stalking. Little did he know if he hadn't been heading to her, she'd have headed to him. Well, she would have if she'd been able to pull her courage out of her ass.

She'd followed the damn rules all her life, and whether any of this made sense or not, she was going with her instincts, or rather hormones, on this one. Her gut screamed this man was far more than just your average guy. Something told her he was a noble and honorable man who, if nothing else, had saved her ass.

"What is your name?"

"Be…Beth Sloan." Oh, my God, she'd just frigging squeaked. Her weak-sounding voice irritated her, as well as the fact she was acting more like a damn schoolgirl than the competent woman who should be grilling the large, nearly naked man for information on where she was and how she could get home. Or at the very least, who he was and what he wanted. Okay, maybe just who he was, since what he wanted seemed pretty damn clear. But oy, her mouth grew dry with each heavy step he took.

Her skin tingled, her ears rang, and strange black dots blurred her vision. Then, for no rhyme or reason, everything around her began to spin. Later she'd wonder why, and assume the heat—and by heat she meant all the forms of heat—had gotten the better of her. So much seemed to be happening in such a short span of time. The hunt with Robby, getting lost and the overwhelming urge to jump the man before her. When the strange feeling passed a few moments later, she buried her head between her knees, nearly choking on her own drool in the process.

"Are you unwell?"

"No. Just a dizzy spell, I'll be fine." She was thankful he must have assumed her jerky reaction from the dizziness, but hell no, he had himself to thank for her quick head to knees move. She'd done it to buy time to help yank her wits and jaw back in place.

He stood right in front of her, and she knew without looking in a mirror her face covered every varied shade of red imaginable, as her position left her nose to, uh, cock with him. And damned if the thing didn't keep bobbin' up and down as if waving hello to her. Though she was no virgin, she was also no slut. She'd seen enough penises, whether in person or online to know the difference between large versus wow, and holy shit, he was generously blessed.

What the hell did one say when placed eye to eye in the most literal sense? Finding no words forthcoming, she did the last thing she'd planned and giggled. Oh, yeah, perfect reaction. She must look like a complete boob right now. Her stomach twisted and turned in several different directions at once, and it took all she had to stifle the nervous giggles fighting for more airtime.

"My pants were in need of drying," he stated, eyebrow arching questioningly at her nervous laughter.

He obviously was aware where her attentions had centered. She watched, dazed and bedazzled, as he stalked even closer, stopping to kneel before her. Kind eyes, yet assured actions, as if he knew how nervous he made her.

Gazing deeper into his eyes, she caught a slight glint reflecting back, and knew though he understood her wariness, he also acknowledged her physical reaction to him.

She wanted him. She knew it. He knew it.

Just once, she'd like to let go and do something wild and impetuous. Spur of the moment without dragging in all the "what ifs" and overanalyzing the situation to death.

When he knelt, pushing her knees out to the sides to make room for him, she didn't try to push him away, nor did she even turn her head. Instead, she held his fiery, determined gaze and matched it with a fire of her own.

Desire and intent flew between them as the need and nature of the moment, so basic and pure, overwhelmed them. His lips brushed across hers, and the knots in her stomach fled, replaced by a strong, pulsing heat coursing through her. His tongue pushed past her parted lips and she opened wider in greeting as her hands drew up to his large, strong shoulders. His kiss deepened to the point she thought breathing an overrated inconvenience. And when his rough, leathered hands brushed against her stomach, grasping the hem of her tee, she instinctively stiffened a bit.

A small inner part of her still warned, *Wrong. Stranger. Run.*

*

He drew back, pausing as he sensed her confusion. Though many called him a monster, he would never harm a woman. He saw the apprehension flickering within her eyes as she seemed to search for something within him.

"What is it you want? Do you require something?" He barely held back the primal urge to take her, claim her, and mark her as his, though she wasn't and could never be.

After only a moment of uncertainty, during which he saw her battle her inner sensibility, did she answer him with a throaty yet confident, "You."

He loved her bashfulness as she began worrying on her lower lip. Something so innocent, yet utterly seductive as it pulled his gaze to the now-plumped pout. Her pink tongue darting back and forth teased his mind with erotic imagery of where else he'd like to see that tongue of hers.

"You are sure of this? Once started, I may not be able to refrain again," he warned through teeth clenched tight, barely hanging on to the little bit of restraint he currently had.

She nodded, yet her body trembled beneath his palms, he hoped in anticipation and not fear.

Moss reached down and encircled her waist, lifting her from her crouch on the bed before bending forward and planting a mind-numbing kiss on her mouth. His mind spun from the intensity and this time, when he grabbed the hem of her shirt, she didn't tense up. Instead, she lifted her arms above her head to assist in its welcomed riddance.

He trailed his tongue from her mouth to the hollow of her neck where he continued his gentle nips until reaching the front clasp of her bra. Her erotic sighs were like music to his ears, urging him onward.

Never before had he experienced this kind of vulnerability—the urgency of wanting her to feel everything he was, from the raging desire to the intense need for her to understand who and what he truly was.

*

Beth watched as sculpted shoulders bunched and beads of sweat rolled down, catching in the many golden, muscled crevices of his body. He appeared to be fighting to hold part of himself back. Quivers rocked his body, and she felt like a goddess taking her god to the brink. He turned predatory as his calm façade fled and sheer urgency surfaced. If he wanted it rough, wanted to grab her ankles, spread her wide and plunge in, hello, that worked for her. She wanted all he offered, however he offered.

She gasped in surprise when teeth tore through the front clasp of her bra, leaving the silken remnants to fall to her sides. Her bared breasts swayed from their sudden release. No sooner had she recovered from the shock than his hot mouth latched onto one now very sensitized nipple.

Her pleasured mewls elicited an almost animal-sounding growl from him. Her head lolled back as he suckled one breast then the other, each time lightly blowing across them so that the contrast from cool to hot was near unbearable. He seemed to take delight in her responses and gave both tight buds lavish attention.

He tore his mouth away like she was a succulent pleasure. Moss recaptured her mouth as his hands made quick work of her khaki shorts. God love drawstring shorts, she thought as they swiftly fell around her combat-booted feet. She was awed when he somehow managed to toe off first one of her boots then the other while his mouth and hands never left their explorative paths along her body.

She went with his every urge and found herself lying back across the bed as he knelt before her again. His eyes sparkled as he took in the sight of her sheer black thong, and she thanked the karma gods she'd chosen the pretty panties over the comfy, ugly ones she'd thought about donning for her trek in the swamp. He fingered underneath the band, almost as if he'd never seen one before. No way a dude this damn hot had never been with a woman wearing a thong.

Grasping the little bows adorning both sides of the sheer fabric covering her mound, he gently tugged until the delicate little things came unbound. The last obstacle shielding him from front-row seating at her bare body quickly flittered away. Now nothing stood between them except for the funky pink polka-dot socks she'd tossed on that morning.

They were skin-to-skin, male to female, and she savored his musky scent.

He placed a hand on each of her knees and gently coaxed them open, never losing eye contact with her as he teasingly lowered his head.

She watched, breath held as his eyes hungrily drank in the bare sight of her. His pupils dilated and his own breath grew ragged. Never before had a lover brought her to this level of being aroused this fast on simple foreplay alone.

Something in him screamed wild, untamed, and dangerous and she reveled in it.

Chapter Four

A gasp escaped past her lips from the shock of his mouth and tongue working with masterful precision. She sighed when his tongue alternated between long languid laps and fleeting swirls over her little bundle of nerves, lost brain cells when small, gentle nips from blunt teeth added to the symphony he orchestrated. He played her like a finely tuned instrument, as if he knew her inside and out and always had. She had the strangest sense they'd always known each other. Like they'd just found one another again. What else could explain the way she responded to him? The lack of fear, the overwhelming desires?

Stop, don't think. Don't even try to analyze this, she told herself. *Live for now, live for the moment, live to please him, and accept the pleasure he's giving.*

Beth moaned when rough, calloused hands blazed trails across her body, stopping only when they reached her chest. Rough palms kneaded her breasts. He lapped at her creamy center, bringing her to the edge of climax. But when one hand left her aching mound and fingers opened her lower lips while coating them with her juices, lubricating them, before slipping into her…she skyrocketed. When a second finger entered, she came unhinged. The climax hit with a fever she'd never before experienced. Her world erupted around her, sounds and lights taking on new hues as her body trembled in sheer delight. No sooner than she'd begun to come back to earth than he poised above her, a hand to each side of her, caging her in for what she expected would be the ultimate in couplings.

*

Moss nipped her clit and delighted as she came unglued under his ministrations. Watched as she bucked and writhed over the old ratty bed—his bed—his own arousal spiking at the erotic sight. A light sheen of perspiration shimmered across her skin. In the dim, moon- and candlelit room, she looked like a masterpiece. An angel amid his dark, watery world. And for now, she belonged to him alone. No one was going to take this moment from him, and God help anyone who tried.

He kneed her legs open farther to accommodate the space he needed. She seemed so small compared to him as her long, graceful legs opened. He took a moment to relish in her giving spirit, leaning back to better appreciate her offering.

The moist, silken folds proved how ready she'd become. Their glistening added visual proof to what his other senses had already established. When his gaze moved back to her face, he caught the cute flush that crept into her cheeks.

Modest and beautiful, he thought, running his thumb through her damp lips before slipping up to her encircle her nub. A smile of satisfaction crossed his face when she arched and whimpered at the act. He reclaimed her mouth, stealing the mewl forthcoming, while continuing to run his thumb around and around the swollen little ball. She thrashed about, reaching for him in futile attempts to bring his body over hers. When she couldn't force him to rise at the moment, her hands clenched the sheet and toes dug into the bed in, he assumed, frustration. He understood the desperation that now fueled her every move, as he felt it too.

*

The sounds of the creaking bed accompanied his weight atop her, and she savored the heavy, hard maleness pushing against her own softness. The broad head of him prodded her, toying with her entrance, and she angled and thrust forward, hoping to force him into her, like right damn now.

Everything went beyond any physical sense of want; she flat-out *needed* more of the primitive release he brought her. She knew her wriggling about only aroused him further. Each time she thought he'd grow no larger, an almost pulse-like sensation stroked her as he continued to lengthen, proving her wrong yet again. Moss was full of surprises. The realization that she was driving this man—no, not just a man, a Hercules-type man—physically crazed, brought her feminine side out, purring.

He stilled as if to verify her readiness, not wanting to rush and, though grateful, she was beyond ready. She grabbed his face, locked eyes with him, and wrapped a leg around his waist to pull him closer while rocking her pelvis into his. That little assurance seemed to send him over the edge, and he thrust.

The force of the initial entrance was powerful enough she was pushed up the bed. Not bad except for scooting her farther away from him, but he quickly rectified that problem by wrapping one arm about her waist, anchoring her to him, keeping her immobile as he began thrusting with obvious pent-up vigor.

She tensed a tad as her walls stretched to accommodate his large girth. The exquisite sensation caused her to gasp as it rode the border between pleasure and pain, with pleasure a rapid winner.

Instinctively she arched, her sensitive nipples brushing against him. The skin-to-skin contact added to her euphoric state. She continued rocking her hips, matching him thrust for penetrating thrust as she held tight to those rock-hard biceps of his.

The sweat they created helped to lube their bodies and create the perfect sliding sensation as they both succumbed to the most basic of all things nature had created. Reaching down, he grabbed her thighs in an attempt to spread her farther. He seemed fueled by her body's visual reactions to him. That he'd freed her inner desires and had her demanding more. Little did he understand, now that she'd sampled what he offered, she'd take nothing less than everything.

"Your scent…so intoxicating…love." He growled, jaw stiff, face intent.

The words went straight to her heart, though she understood things were so intense now that confusion even muddled her mind.

With no warning other than his quick withdrawal, she found herself flipped face down on the mattress, hands clasped above her head, and a powerful arm slung around her waist. He dragged her hips upwards so she ended up on her knees, ass up, with him draped across her backside. She moaned her approval of the change, which in this position gave him all control and would allow for deeper penetration.

And oh, hell, how he took advantage of it.

He accommodated her every unspoken desire as if reading her mind. Beth thought for sure there were times he went so deep, he touched her womb. Between his blessed size and the primal positioning, she lost count of how many orgasms he'd brought her.

As he pumped rapidly, his fingers dug into her hips, keeping her firmly anchored. "Please…" she begged.

"Please what?" He sounded raspy, edgy, demanding.

"Don't, can't breathe, no—don't—stop." She couldn't think straight as her body hit boundaries she hadn't known it had. Everything was too much and not enough all at the same time. He had more stamina than the Energizer Bunny; she stifled the urge to thank him and tell him he was the best lover she'd ever had.

And they weren't even done yet.

*

The fevered pitch of Beth's moans sounded like a heartbeat in Moss' soul as he slammed home repeatedly, thrusting a little harder each time, pounding into her as though he couldn't get enough. He fought back the overwhelming urge to release, opting to savor each moment with her.

Her tight warmth sheathing him made him all the harder. Never had any woman unleashed his beast as she did. It was as if she were the key to unlocking the secrets surrounding the arrival of his current cursed state of being. She was unique in so many ways, and his beast recognized her and raged to mark her as *his*. Strong and self-reliant, yet he sensed a wisdom far beyond her youthful demeanor.

Could he hope she was the fated one to release him from his curse? Or was it too much to hope for such a miraculous thing? What he wouldn't give to walk among society and not have to remain hidden in the shadows of the night. Would he remember what it was like free of the swamps, his only residence in all this time, away from the only friends he had? Namely, the many swamp creatures like him, who society feared and shied away from. Even killed when opportunity arose.

Releasing her hands, he reached around her collarbone and, with gentle pressure, urged her body upwards. He nuzzled her neck, cupping her pert breasts, and tweaked her nipples enough to elicit a startled but pleasant response. The shudders that followed prompted his continued nipple play. He rolled the firm buds between thumb and forefinger until he had her bucking her hips back against him in a wild frenzy. He angled her to half lying, half upright and still on her knees, which was a good position to grant him access to her entire body. No part of her was off limits now. He attempted to slow the pace, wanting to relish every moment of their union, not wanting it to end. Especially when faced with the real possibility of having to watch her walk away.

He forced her head to the side as his tongue sought and dueled with hers. One hand roamed over her front, finding and plucking the tight buds adorning her breasts while his cock, still deeply embedded within her, pumped with frantic need. Flesh slapping flesh sounded through his small abode, as did the strong smell of sex and his keen sense of both ignited a hailstorm of sexual need from him.

He saw a puzzled expression ever so briefly cross her face, when her eyes fluttered open and she caught his partial change in her peripheral vision. Prayed that when spent, she wouldn't remember what she would think she saw, and instead would focus on the raptures they'd shared. Hoped, that while he knew she would leave, maybe they'd lie together a while basking in the sweaty glow of after-sex release.

His reptilian senses and predatory habits peaked, becoming more aggressive with each little mewl she made. His claws extended as he held her very carefully, as in his current state it would be far too easy to forget his strength and rip her to shreds. Not something he wanted to risk as he released his piston-like grip on her hips.

He reached up and instead grasped her firmly by her hair, using it as a sort of leverage. He laid his other hand on her back, turned on its side, claws clenched to ensure he didn't accidentally lay so much as a whisper of a scratch on her.

Then her warm core trembled, beginning an onslaught of fast-paced contractions convulsing around his cock, bringing him past the edge of return. Her back arched, then she dropped down onto the bed, her hands fisting frantically in the sheets as her cries of ecstasy ricocheted through the small hut. His male pride ballooned as she rocked backwards on hands and knees, impaling herself faster, harder, and *deeper* upon his throbbing member. Only when the warm wave of her essence creamed over him did he let go and revel in the release of his own built-up explosion.

Spent, he pulled her down with him on the tattered but welcoming bed, where they stayed silent but well sated, curling into one another with newfound intimacy.

*

Beth delighted in pure feminine satisfaction when she'd caught what sounded like a cross between a hiss and roar escape Moss just before his warm seed shot into her. The sound of their blended orgasms had carried on the swamp's breeze as the sudden sounds of night creatures mysteriously sprang to life. The crickets' chirping amplified, as did the strange, guttural barks of the alligators. Owls seemed to be hooting loud messages as they joined in the swampy chorus. It was as if the entire swamp had burst to life. If she'd been alone it might have been a little creepy, even bothersome, but right now, and with Moss, it emulated the joyous sound of life being celebrated. Like nature had blessed their union herself.

After her heart rate returned to normal and she found her voice again, Beth wondered whether to ask Moss about what she'd seen. She wasn't crazy, and she was fairly certain she had good eyesight, or so she'd been told during her last exam. But for all that, she could have sworn his pupils had become a little more, uh, slit-like? And there been a sudden sharpness to his teeth that hadn't been there before, and his tongue had seemed, oh, thinner, faster, as it hit all the right places and then some. Like it had been forked?

But that was impossible; she'd just been overheated, way too revved up. *Right?*

That would explain the amazing mind-blowing *skills* he'd expended on her down south. *Oh, get a grip, girl, you're just freaking out over a bout of seriously fantastic sex.*

"Moss?" she whispered, voice still tinged with the lazy edge of satisfaction.

"Hmm?"

"How did you find me? You know, out here in the middle of the swamp like you did?"

She couldn't help but find his silence a bit unsettling. She sensed him debating how to answer the question, but wasn't sure what he had to debate about. She wanted to push, make him answer, but deep down she feared the truth and decided to wait patiently.

"I live close by and heard all the commotion you caused."

"I wasn't making any commotion," she countered. Okay, she did scream that one time, but that had been a good bit before he showed up.

Again she met awkward silence. What was he hiding, and did it really matter? Yeah, she'd heard of vampires, werewolves and shifters, knew there was a truth somewhere about them. But what she'd seen wasn't vampiric in nature nor did it even remotely resemble a wolf. The features held more *reptilian*-like qualities.

She pushed a little harder. "So, you heard me? All the way from here?"

"I do not always stay here."

"Oh? Where do you live then?"

Silence.

"Not much of a talker, are you?" she stated more to herself than him.

"I...I do live here." He waved his hands about, seeming to mean more than just the cabin. "But I was returning when I heard you." His voice was a bit stiff. He rose from the bed to stand in the rays of moonlight the glassless sills provided.

"Here as in this swamp, or here as in this cabin?" Though she said cabin, she did so loosely. The place was quite primitive, yet very soothing at the same time. Something about being here in the swamp, with him, felt magical and right.

Her mind skittered off its current path when his rear end drew her gaze. The man was one giant, walking muscle as exemplified by the hard lines that ran the length of his sculpted backside...and front side, for that matter. He stepped farther into the moonlight and when he did, she noticed what appeared to be a tattoo of sorts spreading out over his chest and curving around his body. It shimmered and seemed almost iridescent, its bluish green color replicating the appearance of scales. The transformation didn't end, as he turned facing her and she caught those beautiful, moss-green eyes glowing. He was shifting right before her eyes.

Chapter Five

Okay, this was where most people, *sane* people, would have run away screaming. Instead, Beth thought about how beautiful he appeared. Beautiful in a brooding, sexy, wild unique animal kind of way. Though what kind of animal exactly, still remained a mystery.

"Both," he answered, solemn and grim sounding.

He turned and started toward her. The moonlight cascading around him created a dazzling halo effect. His golden body, toned, taut, and bare, sent her overactive libido stirring once more. She caught his heavy sac drawing up tight, as clearly he too grew eager for more play. His slow, tantalizing gait was teasing and powerful. She licked her lips in anticipation and caught the flare in his gaze, his staff rising again in apparent appreciation of the subconscious act, thick, long, and still glistening from their recent joining.

"I should tell you. Pregnancy nor disease is an issue with me."

She hadn't even thought about that. So swept away with the man and magic of the moment. Her insides twisted at how irresponsible she'd acted, though she had detected something, almost mystical about him.

"And why is that?" She asked hoping he'd open up.

Beth couldn't begin to fathom how in the hell she was this turned on so soon after the best, most intense sex of her life. Yet her breasts weighed heavily while her nipples tingled, and she grew slick again at the erotic sight of him. Desire rolled through her in waves so strong she trembled in anticipation.

"I am not quite human."

"Um, yeah, I had kinda noticed."

He watched her through hooded eyes, as if expecting her to turn tail and run. *Not.* "You are not disgusted by this or afraid of me?" He sounded shocked but relieved and puzzled all at the same time.

"Should I be?" Though she asked, she already had her answer.

"Most would be. Most have been, as maybe you should be." A deep sadness laced his words.

"Well, I am not most, and don't want to be," she reassured him.

No, she hadn't lost her mind; she'd just met many humans she wouldn't call human. So cold and vicious by nature, even assigning them to the animal kingdom seemed unfair. Every day papers across the globe wrote about them. They carried names like serial killer, rapist, murderer.

Instinct told her Moss fit neither category.

Brazen in her current nude state, she closed the gap between them; her nipples brushed him as she came to stand toe to toe with him. Though she rather liked this wanton, slut-puppy side of herself, she hadn't realized it even existed.

She brought her hands to rest on either side of his beautiful yet masculine face and made him look her in the eyes. They stood in a standoff of sorts. More than anything, she needed him to understand she didn't fear him. If he had an inkling of the many things *she* wanted to do to *him*, he might be the one running.

"Moss, I don't care what you are or aren't. I can sense *who* you are."

His hand came down to cup her face, his thumb stroking her bottom lip. He asked, his voice sinfully deep, "And who or what do you think I am?"

"You are a kind, compassionate, and gentle man, Moss." Truthful, yet firm enough she hoped it penetrated his thick skull.

"What makes you so certain when we've just met?" he asked, voice tight, eyes slitted half shut, skeptical.

Though he'd posed it as a question, his voice hinted at confusion. As if he couldn't believe her but wanted to. Begged for a rational answer, like something he'd been searching for, yet hadn't found.

She didn't understand how she knew she told him the truth; she just instinctively understood her words to be true. He was a rare and genuine man, something almost impossible to find in this day and age. Yet out here, in this godforsaken, hot, mosquito-infested swamp, she'd found one such man.

Of course, nothing good in life came without a catch. His just happened to not be one hundred percent human. Hell's bells, he already met five out of the six must haves on her list. He was hot and had already proved it, for starters; he loved nature and the outdoors, he was gentle, smart, and an animal in bed.

In her opinion that last one should get two points, since he had the whole animal sex thing down—in more ways than one.

As for her old required number six—job and/or money? Who the hell cared when he'd met all the others? She sure didn't. She'd learned long ago, money didn't and couldn't buy you happiness.

"Because you have such a gentle aura encircling your soul, Moss. You have the strength of ten men and don't abuse that power," she answered, breathless at being so close to him in the undressed state. Screw propriety, or what most would call slutty—she wanted him again. She wanted this stranger with a passion that, as far as she could tell, wouldn't be sated any time soon. Much like a weary traveler lost in the Mojave Desert searching for water, she sought release with him and went with her instincts.

Gathering her courage and going up on tiptoes again, she brushed her lips across his. The kiss was soft and gentle but with the slow, steaming velocity of a pressure cooker about to blow its top. She suckled his bottom lip, the only part of his mouth she could reach, nibbling until he rumbled beneath her hands splayed on his chest. She moved lower, to his nipples, where she repeated the process. A suck, nip, and swirl of her tongue until she heard the slight growl. His cock did a jig against her belly, and she took immense pride in knowing she caused these reactions from him.

By God, but he tasted like heaven and fucked like hell. Hard and wild with a seemingly insatiable stamina. Where and how got his energy she hadn't a clue, but if it could be bottled, he'd put all those energy drink companies out of business. His body was taut and tight under her exploring hands, and she couldn't seem to keep her nails out of his flesh as she preened and pawed, leaving angry red trails in her nails' wake. Moss didn't seem to care, or maybe he did, but not in a bad way. She couldn't help it; she was reacting to his feral responses. He seemed to bring out the animal in her.

She blazed a lowering trail with her lips and tongue down the path of his ripped body. Tracing every ridge of every ab, pausing only once to glance up when she realized exactly how hard she had raked her nails across his body. She saw no pain etched in his fine features. Quite the contrary—what she saw reflected back from him screamed rock-hard need. Need for release and the desire for her mouth to continue until she reached her ultimate goal, which, by the way he gazed down on her lowering body, was his ultimate goal as well.

"*Bethhhhhhh,*" he groaned as his head lolled back and his body all but vibrated. The gritted, gruff sound sent shivers streaking across her bared flesh. It demanded, yet pleaded for the promised release. His muscles twitched in barely contained restraint, and that restraint only added fuel to the fire burning deep.

When she reached her prize, she settled down onto her knees and grasped him in both hands, still awed at his length and girth. Working two hands simultaneously, she manipulated him so that her hands almost covered his entire length. She slowly alternated movements, going first upwards in a sort of sliding, twisting movement until reaching his base, then repeating the process back up his shaft, circling its blunt, silken head. Grunts and hisses became all the encouragement she needed.

When she took pity upon him and slowly covered him with the heat of her mouth, she thought his legs almost buckled from beneath him. She wet her lips and ran her tongue down and over his length, lubricating him with her mouth and tongue before opening wide to work him in. It took some effort, but she managed most of him before drawing downward to swirl her tongue around the head of his shaft. He was much larger than most and proved quite challenging to take too deeply, but damn if she wasn't going to at least try.

His hands tangled in her hair as he grasped her head and pulled in time with his thrusting hips. She savored the ecstasy of the moment. Wow. She was a bit relieved when he seemed to catch himself from becoming too aggressive, refraining from what would have been an awkward moment to say the least. Considering the size of him—hell, she would have had to be rushed to an emergency room. She really didn't want to explain to any doctors how her tonsils had become dislocated.

His hands were still in her hair, fisting it by handfuls, but he didn't thrust or forcibly hold her in place. Instead he gave her freedom of movement to suck and pull, nip and lick.

As she attempted to get her fill of his unique taste, she used one hand to squeeze and carefully roll his drawn sac, loving each and every ragged breath he took, floating in the exquisite thought that she held this much power over him.

Her. Plain Jane *Beth*, caused this gorgeous, wild, erotic man to tremble like putty in her ministrations. It was such a womanly feeling to be able to give such pleasure.

Not until his body stiffened and his shaft seemed to swell did he pull her away. He looked as though he were trying not only to catch his breath but also to hold back his release. She saw him struggling to regain control of his body. Watched his lids close, brows furrow, sweat bead, and breathing go from uncontrolled and ragged to smooth and even.

Running her nails over his muscular thighs, she kissed the inside of each thigh and noted the beautiful tattoo she'd seen earlier had spread to cover almost his entire body.

Its iridescent details enhanced his every feature, belaying a strange, erotic, and hypnotizing glow. Staring left her dazed and edgy with a need that clawed deep in her gut. She noted he appeared no more in control than she, as the tattoos seemed to cast a spell that drew them into a sexual frenzy.

He grabbed her, and her feet left the floor. She had no choice but to wrap her long legs about his firm, sweat-sheeted hips, clinging on for what was shaping up to be the ride of a lifetime. His lips claimed hers, no longer gentle or controlled, just hungry and demanding. His hands went under her ass, his grip fierce, and the way their bodies slipped against each other was pure heaven. She wanted to scream, maybe hiss—she wasn't sure of anything anymore. Beth let go of all inhibitions and allowed her instincts to guide her. Each slide of their bodies drew her core closer; he'd almost entered her twice now. His cock slipped between her folds and began the initial stretch, then his next step took him farther away. His slow play was driving her insane.

"Now," she pleaded, voice shaking with need.

He mumbled something but did not heed her call; instead he continued walking them toward the moonlight and the open window, stopping to set her upon the sill. Out of habit she threw her legs down to steady herself. But the problem was, there was no way her legs would hold her at this stage of the game. Her body was on fire, and raw hunger brought forth primal urges to bite and scream. Sink her teeth in his flesh, taste him, ride him. She didn't want gentle—she needed hard, rough, and now, damn it.

"Moss-can't-need-must, please...now." Something old and primitive in nature drove her every move. Told her what he wanted and needed and though he'd just placed her on the windowsill, she knew he needed to dominate, and it was within her power to submit.

In a show of submission, she hopped down off the window ledge, whirled around and grasped the sill before her, leaning outwards, elongating her body and tilted her ass upwards in offering. Exposing her core, proving she was ready for him, in a most basic position. She almost laughed from giddy nervousness as she seductively pivoted her hips back and forth, desperately hoping the slight swaying would lure him into immediate entry. Her breathing was so ragged she feared she'd hyperventilate and pass out before obtaining her objective. She was desperate, plain and simple. No more foreplay—here, now, *must have.*

The heat of his body as he sidled up behind her, kicking her legs farther apart, spiked shivers over her. His hands went to her hips as he nudged her entrance, still toying with her. She moaned and tried to nestle back, forcing him to enter. His hands began rubbing up and down her spine, each pass pushing her upper body more downward. She gasped, startled when he plunged a finger in, apparently checking her readiness.

Readiness? Hell, she was so far past ready it wasn't even funny. Lifting her ass as high as she could, she arched her backside before lunging backwards, taking matters into her own hands.

He entered hard and swift, and if not for her death grip on the sill, she most likely would have sailed clear through to the other side. It was glorious. He created a decadent fullness as her body struggled to sheath him in his entirety. He continued filling her as every inch of her shivered in completion. When he lunged into her again, she screamed. Not in pain, but in pure, unadulterated ecstasy. Something changed within her and she suspected within him as well. There was a strong sense of bonding and unity much like how the swamp itself is both beautiful and deadly, yet comes together in harmony to create a magical environment. The moon seemed to adorn the union, gifting them with silvery threads of light that played off his ornate tattoos, visible to her only on the arm snaring her waist.

For each of his voracious thrusts, she braced herself against the sill and luxuriated in euphoric bliss. When he released her hips and snaked an arm around to cup her breast, she glimpsed that the hand, *his* hand, bore claws. These dangerous talons, which she had no doubt could shred her in a moment's haste, ever so carefully began to knead her achy breasts. There was something so erotic about the danger and gentleness of the act.

Rough yet gentle, wild but tame, human but not. Moss was everything right now. One talon-spiked hand wrapped about her waist while the other drew her head back enough she felt his tongue flick against her lips. She parted her eyelids enough to see that his pupils had become oval shaped and his tongue appeared to have split. She reached behind her and ran a hand down his shoulder, and even at her awkward angle, she felt a difference in his skin. Not cold, or scaly—no, more smooth and cool like a seashell. And the visual? Stunning. Rather like that of the beautiful coquina shell. Iridescent with many colorful hues, but the predominant color was that of bluish-green.

Regardless of what Moss might be, he was unique and oh, so damn hot. As her orgasm roared to the surface, he firmly urged her head to the side and laid molten kisses on her exposed neck, lapping and sucking on its hypersensitive skin.

But what he did next startled her in the most pleasant of ways.

Chapter Six

He continued to piston in and out, causing knee-shaking, sigh-inducing friction. She gasped at the slight sting on her neck. The spot he'd been working with such fevered intent. Not painful as no sooner than she felt it…then the world around her exploded into a multitude of sensations and emotions. She trembled from whatever the bite did to her but, at the moment, she didn't care what it was.

The orgasm ripped through her, more powerful than she'd ever thought possible. Colors became more vibrant, clashing together to cause the strangest kaleidoscope.

Yet he wasn't done. Yowza.

She clung to the sill as he continued thrusting into her time and time again, so hard his balls slapped her clit, further enhancing whatever the hell he'd done to her neck. Their grunts, groans and sighs overtook all other sounds around them. Even drowned out the crickets.

"Moss—God, yesssssssss," she screamed out in ecstasy.

Still riding the orgasmic high and unable to form coherent words, she sighed when he turned her around and carried her over to the bed. After setting her down, he climbed in and spooned up next to her, his large body almost cocooning hers in jigsaw-like precision. She was pretty certain that this was what heaven felt like.

His large body cradling hers, so protective and possessive, was a decadent treat, and in no time, she drifted off. For the first time in her entire life, she didn't worry what tomorrow held. Her nightmares were put on hold, all thanks to her handsome new friend and lover, Moss.

*

Beth was so much more than he'd ever dreamed. Real, and here with him, and even if only for the moment…his dream was real.

Hard as he'd tried to refrain from marking her, in the end the beast won the round. The urge to mate and mark overwhelmed any form of self-preservation he'd held. His marking shouldn't affect her in her world, where mortals walked side by side and lazy human males left their women unaccompanied and unprotected. No, when she returned to her world his warning would go unnoticed. He understood someone like Beth would never willingly want to stay in his world, this savage place where only the strong survived. Where alphas ruled, the predators hunted, and only those willing to do whatever necessary lived to see another day.

Yes, he could force her to stay. Take a captive bride, keep her chained to him by day and wrapped around him during the nights. Just the thought made him growl possessively. He wanted nothing more than to howl into the night that he'd found his mate. He felt it as clearly as he'd sensed her, lost and frightened in the swamp, hours earlier.

Her essence, her blood, and her soul called to him in a way that defied logic. Like a song gently carried by the warm swamp winds, bringing her to him.

He hadn't replied to her huskily whispered pleas during their lovemaking with words but instead answered with bodily action, which had seemed more than acceptable to her. He'd spilled his seed into her welcoming body, filling her with his distinct scent. A scent that no doubt would drive all potential suitors and predators away as they would be able to detect with clarity, her claimed status.

Moss watched as Beth slept peacefully, clothed only in the pale moonlight and felt torn in two. He understood tomorrow's new day would have her leaving him to return to the sanctity and safety of her own world, family, and possible lovers.

The thought of some other male placing his hands on her in any intimate way brought his fangs and predatory instincts roaring to the surface. All thoughts of males even being interested in her created images of ripping their throats out while injecting his venom in them, before feeding their worthless, miserable carcasses to the many hungry and territorial gators infesting his home here in the swamp.

Heart heavy, he acknowledged staying with him would be unfair and too dangerous for her. Come morning, he would escort her safely to her home then leave her in peace. It was too much to have hoped she held the key to unlocking the curse, which held him here in the swamp. The watery place he now called home, with the creatures he now considered family, for they'd been the only constant companions he'd had for many long years now. He'd looked for any signs she held the secret. But if she indeed held such a key, she wasn't aware of the fact. To ask her to go into such a dark and evil place to attempt to find it was not something he would ask of her. She might not be his, but she was special, and he would forever hold her in his memories and heart.

Beth would never experience the darkness surrounding his existence, and he would take solace in the knowledge of this. He wished her only peace and happiness. If nothing else, he'd go to his grave content that at least once in his miserable existence, he'd done right by someone.

He brushed a kiss across her forehead as sleep carried her farther away.

"Sleep, love, for no harm shall come to cross you while you are here."

*

Beth awoke to sunlight filtering in through cracked wooden shutters. Nice—the windows featured no glass, but by gosh, they sure as hell sported shutters. Strange, to say the least, she mused, looking around for Moss.

Sitting up, she realized she hadn't been this relaxed in years. The old, lumpy bed hadn't bothered her at all. She felt like a goddess at the moment. She stretched her bare legs and noted the faint tenderness between her thighs. But damn if last night wasn't worth every ache and pain nagging her this morning. She was sated in both body and soul, and as a result, Beth wanted to dance about the drafty old place—yes, even naked.

"Moss?" Beth yanked the sheet up and wrapped it about herself as she headed out to the porch. There were no other hidey holes around for the big guy to be.

"Hey, Moss, where are you?" she called as she pulled open the rickety screen door expecting to find him standing there, but found only a humid, vacant porch.

She scanned the swamp, noting the gorgeous way the rising sun reflected off the jade-green waters, but still found no sign of Moss. She lingered, absorbing the beautiful sight while soaking up the warm rays of the sun against her bare skin.

The smell of fresh-brewed coffee made its way into her newly awakened, still-groggy senses. She turned back to the cabin and found an old fashioned, blue speckled kettle hanging over the fire by a wire. On the small wobbly wooden table just next to the fire, sat one lone cup. God love a man who knew to have coffee ready before leaving in the morning. Only after taking two large sips from the best damn cup of coffee in the world did she noticed her clothes. They appeared clean and were folded neat and tidy on a small footstool by the bed.

Not seeing anything even remotely like a bathroom, she dropped the sheet she'd slung about her and dressed while doing the potty dance.

When in Rome. She leaned her rear end over a rusty old coffee container she found stacked in a corner, appearing to be garbage, and aimed well.

After she'd polished off the remainder of the coffee, she realized Moss didn't appear to be coming back any time soon. She was more than a little hurt—stunned, even. She'd thought there'd been sparks between them last night. Something far more than just an amazing, mind-blowing, one-night stand. She must have been sorely mistaken. It wouldn't be the first time she'd made this kind of mistake. But he'd seemed so different.

It just didn't make any damn sense. Why the hell would he have disclosed his secret if he didn't intend to stay close? Why trust her at all? Maybe he simply didn't care anymore if the legend of the Bog Monster, his secret, got out. That, in fact, no Bog Monster existed. Only a swamp man. A very natural, organic, swamp Adonis with rippling muscles and tawny skin…and, uh, all his other very well-endowed features.

Had she done something wrong, said something offensive? She couldn't think what. Last night had contained very few words and far more action.

As she waited for what seemed an eternity, but truly had been only an hour or so, her heart sank with each passing minute.

And then she heard her name whispered. Though the sound was distant, she clearly made it out.

She headed back outside when the voices drew closer. She recognized one as belonging to her deadbeat brother. Wow, only an entire night and a half to find her? She should be impressed he hadn't given up, gone home, and gotten himself too inebriated to even notify anyone of her absence. He wasn't the type to have ever been called bright, not even remotely so.

"Robby." She waved her arms almost reluctantly to grab his attention. He and his friends paddled up to the dock, the canoe rocking precariously.

"Thank God. Where the hell have you been? We've been worried sick, and Aunt Grace flipped out on me all damn night," he spat, climbing out to come and meet her on the dock. They almost fell. She really wished they had.

"I got turned around in the swamp fogs last night and got lost. Thank God I found this place," she answered, calm and nonchalant. Nice that her brother was more worried about catching hell from Aunt Grace than over the possibility Beth had been injured or worse.

Well, she hadn't spent the night alone, but she sure as shit wasn't telling Robby that.

"Damn, lucky thing you found this old termite heap." Robby pushed past her and entered the cabin, and she couldn't explain why, but it rattled her as wrong. Like trespassing. This was Moss's place. His private domain, and yet here her brother and his drunkard buddies were just walking in and tossing things about.

When Brian, Robby's oldest friend, ran over and jumped high and hard on the old bed, she lost her temper, snapping at him to get off. The bed, Moss's bed, which they'd snuggled in just hours earlier, nearly broke from the rough abusive treatment. She feared the heathen really would break it and the thought of Moss tossing it out, like he'd apparently done to her, ate a raw spot in her heart.

"Come on, let's head home," she urged, growing livid at the audacity of Robby and his friends' crude behavior.

"Man, check out all the old ancient shit. Hey, Brian, you think any of this old crap might be worth something to old man Withers?" She could see the dollar signs going cha-ching in Robby's greedy little liquored mind.

"Man, it would be sweet if it was. That crazy ole coot loves old junk like this," Brian replied, getting those same greedy dollar signs in his eyes.

"Oh, ow." Moaning, Beth doubled over, gripping the edge of the tiny table as she held her stomach like she was in excruciating pain.

"What's wrong with you?" Robby asked, more curious than concerned. "You're not about to hurl or anything, are you?" He backed up, holding up his arms in a staying motion.

"No. I don't know…maybe? I think I caught something out in the swamp last night."

"Fine, let's head back. We can always come back later and scope the place out," Robby casually replied.

She let the guys lead the way. As she turned to shut the door, she fought back tears from the horrid sense she would never see Moss again. That her Bog Man was gone, and she'd never get the chance to tell him how she felt. Or about the crazy dream she'd had last night. So vivid and real, while filling her with hope and questions for him. If only he'd stayed and given her a chance to tell him about it.

Hell, she wasn't even sure he would have believed her. Many didn't believe in the power of dreams or precognition.

Ever since she was a child, she'd dreamt of a man whose back appeared to glow. She'd never seen the face of the man, only sensed his gentle soul and caught the peculiar glow of what she guessed were tattoos on his back. She hadn't put two and two together until this morning. When, after having the dream again, she remembered that just before she fell asleep, when Moss had turned to climb into bed, the moonlight hit his tattoos. How the combination was so bright, the tats almost glowed. She awoke excited and a bit nervous to explain why she'd thought he felt so familiar.

Giving up her battle, she let the tears flow, streaking down her face as she settled into the canoe, longingly searching the area one last time for her mysterious Bog Man.

Chapter Seven

After a full day of sulking about, Beth's anger at the so-called Bog Man kicked in. How dare he walk away like she'd been nothing more than a one-night stand, regardless of how damned good the *one night* may have been? Yeah, highly pissed described her current emotion. After all these years of dreaming of him, and he was nothing more than your typical SOB male out looking for an easy lay.

She wadded up yet another fouled attempt at trying to type her thesis. She'd tried to tune out her anguish enough to proofread, but each time she printed and read, another typo sprang up from the page as if taunting her at her failure. She tossed the crumpled paper and missed the wastebasket. *Pfft, freaking perfect.* Working or studying right now was slap out of the question, as too many questions lingered regarding Moss. Her mind kept flittering back to when the dreams—or visions, as she thought of them now—had first begun.

They'd been downright horrifying at first. But as she grew older, curiosity outweighed the fear. Mostly about the one that reoccurred so often. Later on, one of her professors had suggested the dream stood for something her subconscious wanted her to deal with. Possibly an underlying fear of being left alone, which did tend to make sense, since she always got a bit jittery when becoming lost.

Through the years, the nightmare had sort of reshaped itself. More accurately, her maturing mind did. She only remembered the fear being replaced by something else. Something more erotic in nature. Of course, by this time her raging hormones and lack of dates more likely explained the change.

The dream always started the same. The sense of terror, her trembling, lost in a swamp at night. Frantically trying to find her way out while a strange, green, hazy, thick mist with an evil glow rolled in, encasing her. The panic of suffocating would hit. As if on cue, a strange, mysterious chanting would start. Like someone taunting her in an evil, singsong way. Hostility was evident in every sung syllable. Even though she never, even to this day, could make out the words, she always sensed the evil nature of them.

Then the dream would slowly morph into her being in a strange cavern, her sheer, white gown plastered to her, making wading through the bogs quite difficult. Within the cavern, she would find a magnificent home. Not an average home where one found normal household fixtures and furniture. No, this one was extraordinary and exotic.

A beautiful, black baby grand piano sat in one corner. Beautiful artwork ornamented the cave walls, and Persian rugs, sure to have been made of the finest threads, covered the floors. Even a crystal chandelier adorned the entry. She always had an *Alice in Wonderland* feeling when first entering the chamber.

Then the dream changed one day. Where once she'd only been able to glimpse the unique home, the dream grew, became longer, more alluring, and far more erotic in nature.

A figure would emerge from the shadows, large and at first appearing menacing. Later, when the shadowy figure stepped into the candlelight, the form of a man would become clear. A very large and quite naked man. One hundred percent naked, and a true vision of a perfect male specimen. The vision never allowed a clear view of his face—only his glorious body covered in strange, erotically placed tattoos.

He never spoke, and Beth didn't think he was even aware of her presence. However, he always seemed to scan the area as if looking for something or someone. An aura of sadness and longing surrounded him. Though his eyes searched, he never spoke, nor did she, as she remained too enraptured to dare make a sound. His demeanor seemed to beckon her.

The sense of foreboding radiating from him always left her quivery from its sheer intensity. He'd been hurt. Betrayed by someone, quite badly, and so he had locked himself away from the world and pain. Beth wanted nothing more than to soothe his aches and hurts away. Longed to run her fingers down the delicious, tawny skin covered in intricate art. Wanted to knead his firm ass in her hands and to run her tongue over the ridges of rock-hard abs. But the dream never allowed such a thing. No sooner that she gathered the courage to approach him, the vision would once again morph, leaving Beth with *her*.

Her being the evil bitch who took the sexy tattooed man's spot.

She, with her midnight black hair and beady black eyes. She who appeared to be around age forty with an intense angry look on her pinched, pissed face. The room changed as well. No longer was it a beautiful cave, but instead she and prune face sat rigidly in a small canoe filled with strange jars and containers of different sorts. Beth had no doubt this was the woman behind the strange chants. Evil clearly hovered around this bitch, and she absorbed it. Ate it raw, relishing every dark morsel.

Unlike the mystery man, Beth knew the bitch sensed her. Beth didn't understand how a freaky vision or possible dream could become real, but this evil woman *knew* she was there. As always, right before the dream ended, the woman turned and stared right at her, shrieking some ungodly, high-pitched sound. A clear and definite warning for Beth to steer clear of the tattooed man.

Then she'd awaken, covered in sweat and drenched in fear. Fear for herself, fear for what lay in her future, and fear for one of the most beautiful men she'd ever seen.

Now, after meeting Moss, she realized the so-called dreams had truly been visions, and somehow she and her bog man were truly tied. She'd been meant to get lost in the swamp, and he'd been meant to find her. Fate had thrown them together for a reason, and she now understood she held the key to something bigger than both of them.

She just wasn't sure what the hell it was. But it was damn sure much larger than just a one-night hookup, regardless of what his sorry ass might think.

She sat there unconsciously tapping her fingers against the desk, deep in thought. Maybe solving the mystery of what the visions meant, who the strange evil woman was, and what exactly her ties to Moss were, would help lead her to Moss and get him to open up and trust her. At the very least, she could find him to grant her closure of sorts.

No, she wasn't so desperate as to beg, but the more she thought about Moss's peculiar actions, the more she was beginning to feel that Moss's disappearance wasn't about him wanting a quick *wham, bam, thank you Ma'am,* but rather his fear of being hurt again or betrayed.

If she interpreted the visions correctly, then Moss feared betrayal more than anything else, even loss. She'd have to prove she was trustworthy, and that she'd never hurt him.

Who'd hurt him so badly, and how had he come to be the way he was? Part man, part reptile? The woman in the visions was connected, and Beth wondered if the swamp witch of old legends might be true. It would make sense.

Her aunts had always warned her and Robby as children about venturing into the swamp. But their backyard *was* the swamp, and to forbid anyone from going too close to the woods was an asinine, unrealistic request. So why then had her aunts been so adamant about them never venturing too close or too deep?

Beth grabbed her notepad and jotted down some quick notes. First, she needed to call Aunt Grace. Next, she should contact Professor Jacobs, whose hobby was urban legends. And to round up the research, she needed to go to the library and attempt to read about when the legends of the Bog Monster had first started.

She'd leave Moss alone for now. She'd work on solving the mystery, and once she'd solved it, she would return to the swamp, find her bog man, and help him heal…emotionally.

Chapter Eight

Almost a week had passed since Moss's sudden departure from her life and she still hadn't learned all that much about him, or rather, his alter ego, the Bog Man. Whoever the hell had penned the quote "time flies" could kiss her ass. For her, time had frozen. Minutes crept by like days as she'd attempted to unravel the mystery surrounding Moss only to keep coming up empty-handed and frustrated.

Her professor, claiming to be current with most urban legends, had only read of the legend in local papers, but knew nothing about the origin. Yes, she'd discovered countless articles about him in the library's database, but nothing more informative than the typical "Billy Bob experienced brush with death in the swamps, having had a run-in with the legendary man-eating Bog Monster."

Man-eater, her ass. He ate…shit, even thinking of what he did and how made her blush.

Lucky for her, Aunt Grace was due back in town any time. If anyone had information about the town, legendary or not, it would be Aunt Grace.

*

Moss hated having to meet the dangerous old bitch. But when the she-demon herself called, he had no choice but to answer. She'd even sent him a graphic vision of what would befall Beth should he attempt to avoid responding.

Yes, he'd made numerous attempts to ignore her calls, which launched pinpricks of apprehension across his skin and twisted his insides. No matter how he'd tried to avoid responding in the past, Beth's safety took priority now; he had to obey.

Skillfully, he skimmed through the murky waters until he arrived at her dark abode. He forced himself toward the door. Her evil laugh proved her aware of his torment. No matter—he would do whatever he needed to do in order to keep Beth safe. It mattered not that he'd never be with her again, even for one lone night. To ensure her happiness and safety would be well worth all the evil bitch would call on him to do and endure. He turned the rusty knob and pushed open the ancient door. Octavia stood at the hearth, as a fire raged strong enough that a blast of heat assaulted him with his first steps into her weathered, but spacious cabin.

The witch handed him a tarnished brass goblet containing some strange, smoking brew. "Drink," she commanded.

Warily, he accepted the goblet, already knowing the drink would be laced with something. With what had yet to be determined. But he had no choice. He drained the contents in one gulp.

"Come, Moss. Kiss me," she beckoned, dropping her robe. The sheer material floated to the floor around her feet, exposing her nude body.

Moss staggered backwards, shaking his head for clarity, repulsed by the images she broadcast at him. His surroundings began to become fuzzy and unclear as she shook her head and body in a fierce fashion. Back and forth she shook, hair flying about. Confusion took hold of Moss as she went from being a witch to an exact replica of...

Beth.

As she slunk toward him, he tried again in desperation to clear his mind. He *knew* it wasn't Beth, but everything spun so fast, and he continued to see her. Even heard the soft lilt of her voice and the sweet murmurs she'd made during their lovemaking.

Her lips claimed his as those memories overtook him. Of Beth's skin against his, slick with sweat as their bodies rubbed and slid against each other's. Her aroused scent as he pounded into her welcoming, tight, hot sheath. His lips parted, allowing her tongue to engage with his. He needed to taste her again, needed to be balls-deep within her. The heady scent of her desire permeated the air, mixing with his.

Yes, he needed her, and needed her now. He pulled her roughly against him, wrapping her in his bulging arms before backing her toward the wall for support. He didn't stop until her back jarred against the wood.

Rough, too rough. Must be easy.

Reaching down, he urged her thigh over his to allow for easier access. Instead of complying, she pushed back and flipped him around, so *his* back leaned against the wall. Shocked, yet pleased by her sudden aggressiveness, he yielded.

He closed his eyes as her eager hands undid his pants. She jerked them down in one rough, swift movement that freed his engorged cock from the binding restraints. God, he needed to take her, but first he would allow her to explore his body as she wanted.

Finally, her mouth took him. The slow, warm sweep of her tongue had him groaning. Images flashed through his head. Extreme need and desire warped his thoughts as less than gentle ideas flared through his mind. Confusion set in, and he became nervous to touch her. Frightened he'd do what his mind showed him—grab her by the back of her head and force his cock right down her throat. Though aroused, he felt jittery and off.

Beth toyed with him, something far too dangerous for her to be doing right now with such aggressive thoughts racing through him. She ran her teeth around the rim of his cock before then running her tongue over the slit and engulfing him once again.

Moss fought the sense of confusion sweeping through him as well as its accompanying wild compulsions. Struggled against the darkness threatening to take a firm hold. But everything he tried proved futile. Dark erotic images, like none he'd ever thought, consumed him in a tighter grasp. His skin burned as if flames engulfed him and only his release would squelch them.

Almost against his will, his hands dropped to grasp each side of her head as he jerked forward, thrusting his cock deep. He heard her gag as her hands flattened against his thighs. She pushed against him, desperate for freedom. Yet he could not stop—was driven by some all-consuming force. Even as his mind screamed at him to stop, for this was his fragile and beloved Beth. Yet his need for release built as he continued to pump in and out, and as her oh, so hot, tight little mouth stretched to take all of him.

He roared as he exploded. His body jerked as his seed shot down her throat. Only then did the demons release him to view the extent of his rough deed.

Her eyes were swollen, her mouth red from being stretched so forcefully. Worse yet were, her damp, tear-stained cheeks as she lay on her side gasping for air. Her frail body trembled from his abuse and now no doubt in fear of him.

Guilt assaulted him over what he'd done. What he'd forced on her. Losing the energy to fight, he allowed the lethargic aftershocks to consume him. He sank into the darkness, sliding down the wall, in utter despair over his ruthless attack on the woman he loved.

He truly was the monster so many claimed him to be.

*

"What in heaven's good name has spooked you hard enough to be perched up here on my doorstep with that kind of frown?"

Beth looked at her aunt, realizing she must look like complete shit. She took a deep, steady breath, before plowing forward. "I need some of your worldly advice."

Oh, yeah, those words would pique her aunt's interests into helping her before unpacking from her latest gambling trip in Biloxi .

"Pfft. It's man troubles, isn't it? Sweetie, let me tell you. You can't live with 'em, and you sure as hell can't live without 'em. Trust me, I've been alone long enough to understand the latter," she stated with a wink and clucked her tongue.

Yep, Aunt Grace always had the ability to read someone in five seconds flat. You never went to her place when trying to hide something. She could get blood from a turnip, should she decide she wanted to.

"Yes, man troubles it is," Beth rushed out with a heartfelt sigh.

"Well, sweetie, you came to the right aunt. I'll fix us some of my special tea while you tell me all about him. And honey, I mean everything. Don't leave out the juicy good stuff."

By special tea, she meant her signature spiced tea. Earl Grey meet Jack. Jack Daniels.

Leaning over, Beth grabbed the overstuffed suitcase out of her aunt's hand while Grace unlocked her front door. She followed her aunt inside the warm home, hope springing with each step she took. She prayed Grace would be able to help her, as she sensed time was running short.

Chapter Nine

The swamp's numerous frogs croaking coupled with the crickets chirping obnoxiously loud drew Octavia achingly back to the present. She'd allowed Moss to leave as she lay heaped, humiliated, and more than a little angry.

So he wanted to play rough, did he? Well, so be it. Rough he'd receive. She would teach Moss to respect her, fear her, even worship her.

She tapped her finger against the floor as an idea formed. Yes, she knew exactly how to achieve his punishment, thus bringing him to his knees and killing two birds with one lovely little spell.

The Beth woman she'd seen in his memories, whore that she was, would just have to die. But not before being tortured, painfully and long, all in the presence of Moss. Yes, the mere thought of executing her plan almost made up for the brutal assault he'd bestowed on her mouth.

Snatching a towel from the cabinet next to her, she wiped her mouth as she stood on legs still a bit wobbly from the extreme encounter. To say Moss was well endowed didn't come close. He was huge and left her feeling like her jaws had come unhinged.

She made a quick mental note to use less pickerelweed in the next batch of lust-inducing brew.

*

Beth watched as Grace filled a teakettle and turned the antique porcelain knob to high. Her aunt had never aged. She couldn't count how many times they'd been out together and men had hit on her. Her fair hair and light eyes drawing them like bees to honey. Yet never once had her aunt taken any seriously.

She'd smile, make polite chatter and then keep going to wherever she'd been heading. Beth always sensed an underlying sadness behind her aunt's bright eyes and warm smile. As if a long ago, tragedy had left its scars on her soul. Healed, and though faint, the silvery threads were still there. Oddly, Beth had never heard mention of anything horrific happening to her.

"Well, let me see, where do you want me to start?" Beth asked settling in at the kitchen table.

"At the beginning?" Grace suggested with a wise gleam in her eye.

"Well, aren't we ever the wise elder?"

Grace wasn't really old or offended. Beth always teased her overly age-conscious aunt. Grace was classic. She had that old Hollywood natural beauty thing going on but with a most un-classical twist.

Grace had a special knack for reading people instantly. Which was unfortunate for most, if they didn't wish to be read. The sheriff's office even called her in as a consultant at times, though they did so reluctantly, afraid the local media would catch wind of it. Lord help them if the town thought the local boys couldn't handle shit without the need to call in a psychic. It was a small town, where everyone knew everyone and local law enforcement officers came highly revered.

Beth settled into the well-worn wooden chair and accepted the hot, spiced tea Grace handed her before beginning her much-edited tale of becoming lost in the swamp. She purposely left out Moss, and instead concentrated her story on the trouble she had finding her way out. She wove in her theories on the Bog Man legends. Her aunt listened quietly to the entire story, appearing deep in thought.

Finishing her tale, Beth sat back, anxious of what her aunt thought. After several long, silent minutes, Grace shook her head, sighed, and began her own tale.

"A very long time ago your Great-Great Grandmother Mirabelle used to tell bedtime tales of the Bog Monster. According to her, a monster he was not; in fact, she claimed him to be angelic. She credited him with bringing back a group of young campers who had gotten turned around out in the swamp's ever-winding paths."

"He saved them?" Beth asked, awed but not the least bit surprised.

"According to her, indeed he did. And apparently he still does. Many people return from the swamps claiming to have lost their way, and many have claimed to have seen the swamp come alive to show them their way out." Sipping her tea, she told of salvation to those who had been lost and frightened out in the harsh, dangerous swampland. She spoke of grateful parents dropping to their knees in sheer and utter happiness at their children being returned to their arms.

"Is there nothing of who he is or what happened to him?" Beth asked hopefully.

"Honey, you talk like he's real, and you've met him. Is there something you're not telling me?"

There was no point in lying. If anyone would believe her, understand her desperation, that person would be Grace. So she took another deep breath and filled in the gaps of her previous story, leaving nothing out.

Well, almost nothing. She blushed.

"You're in love with him, aren't you?"

"Yes. And I understand how unrealistic and rash it may sound, but…"

"But what?" Wise eyes narrowed, awaiting her answer.

"But there is something about him that calls to me. Beckons me, like our souls are intertwined. Halves that found each other and can recognize it, even if we really don't understand it yet ourselves. I sound crazy, right?" Beth rubbed her temples.

Aunt Grace smiled one of her famous, all-seeing, all-knowing smiles. "Very well, then, you deserve the whole story, don't you?"

Beth sat upright. "Whole story?"

"Yes, the buried part. The part our family has kept mum about for a long time. Too long, in fact." Grace chuckled and added in a hushed whisper. "Yes, the proverbial family skeleton falls out of the closet now."

Beth wasn't sure whether to be intrigued or scared.

"Oh, come now. No reason for such an alarmed expression. You already learned good and well about our certain...ah, shall we say gifts?"

Grace was right. Beth had always known they were all a bit different. Hell, most of the town seemed to shoot curious stares their way, but no one had ever elaborated on the stigma. Grace had a unique gift, which could only be described as insight. According to whispers she'd heard as a child, Great-Great Grandma Mirabelle had been a self-proclaimed witch, and Beth's mother always had a nifty way of stopping things. Beth had dropped a vase once, and miraculously her mother had rescued it before it hit the floor. Thing was, she'd been across the room. Even as a kid, Beth knew her mother couldn't have made it in time—yet she had.

Yeah, her family didn't quite fit the typical *Leave it to Beaver* stereotype. But who was she to complain? They were a laidback, honest, open-minded, colorful bunch of folks. She'd met her share of the so-called "typical" families, who for the most part couldn't stand being in the same room with one another. She'd never have been able to tolerate that sort of family. She loved her quirky but close-knit family and would accept them over the typical family, any day of the week.

"I suppose, yes, I've always suspected we were uh, unique?"

Grace choked on her tea so hard, drizzles of it ran down her nose. "Oh, I love that. Unique. Yes, I suppose that's an appropriate description."

"Okay, back to the story. Do you know who he is?" A strange, panicky feeling nagged Beth, as if Moss's life depended on her solving the mystery. Like some internal clock ticked away, and the alarm was set to go off any minute.

"I'm not one hundred percent certain, mind you, but yes, I'm fairly confident I know who he is, and what happened to him," Grace offered with a sly smile.

"And?" Beth nearly screamed in frustration. "Who do you think he is?"

"Well, sweetie, many years ago a legend began. One told faithfully around these parts from as far back as I can remember, but word of mouth dates the story clear back to the eighteen hundreds. My grandfather told the tale, as did many other grandfathers in these parts, I suspect. It was said to be based on true accounts. You'll have to make up your own mind about that."

Slamming back her hot tea, Beth had a feeling she'd lose the tea and head straight for the "spice" by the time Grace finished telling of Moss's possible tragedy.

"A group of young settlers arrived late one foggy evening to settle down in these parts. Their leader found the safest spot he could, considering it was late and visibility was next to nothing once our famous swamp fogs rolled in. Many were quite unnerved with the chosen spot; however, nightfall decreed they must stop. Word said several protested, nearly violently, urging their young leader to move on, even if just a few more feet. But others had already settled the horses and had begun to bed down in their wagons. The leader, a young husband and father whose name has never been mentioned, had taken charge of the small group upon the untimely death of the original leader. Seems he allowed a few of the older boys to venture out for an evening's constitutional. After asserting they were not to wander far and come swiftly back, he'd settled back and indulged in some much-relished Jameson Irish whiskey."

"What happened?" Beth hurried her, sensing the "but" coming. Something bad must have happened. Behind every great legend was always a greater tale of tragedy.

Chapter Ten

"Well, as I said, the man was young and unaccustomed to liquor and ended up drinking a tad too much. The story goes that when the boys didn't return, his fellow settlers tried to rouse him. They were successful; however, he became ill and indisposed. Irate at his irresponsible behavior, several went searching for the boys themselves. The leader's young wife, feeling somewhat responsible, led the search party out into the dark, unknown swamp, as her husband attempted quick sobriety. She refused to return with the others several hours later after exhaustive attempts turned up none of the missing children.

"When they returned, they angrily blamed their leader for the event. Having finally purged himself of the liquor, he faced the mob, and the frantic cries of the childless mothers sobered him into action. He promised the return of the children and took off in search of the lost boys and his young bride."

"He never found them, did he?"

"Patience," Grace tsk'd. "Hear the story out."

Beth rolled her eyes and barely managed to restrain an exasperated sigh. Yes, she needed to hear the whole story, but at a much quicker pace. The way Grace retold the story left Beth feeling as if she should be sitting around a campfire while some counselor tried to scare the heebie-jeebies out of her.

"The remaining settlers claimed strange, frightening noises erupted through the deafening darkness. Many swore the swamp itself came alive in search of souls to claim. All hopes for the safe return of their lost children waned in those dark, bleak moments. Come morning, however, the young bride of their leader appeared with the rising of the sun. They say she appeared as an angel would, caressed in the rays of a new dawn, and with her were the missing children, all of them. None of the children had any memories of their night lost in the swamp, nor how they came to be back at the camp."

"What happened to the young man? Their leader?"

"He was never to be seen alive again. Many years later, his heartbroken young bride had him declared dead and, according to records, she died a short time thereafter. Her heart, they said, never recovered from the tragedy."

"How heartbreaking. No rumors of what became of him? A gator or bear attack? Someone went looking for him, didn't they?"

"Nope, at least nothing on record. Strangely enough, the settlers claimed no memory of when the children came back. However, locals swore the swamp witch who was rumored to inhabit the area had caused the tragedy. Testimony from locals mentioned the disappearance of young, virile men out hunting in the swamps was a common occurrence. Legend tells that after a bad storm, if you listen close enough to the toads croaking, you can make out the pleas of those lost men begging to come home."

"Uh, toads? You are joking, right? Isn't that a little cliché?"

Grace shrugged, uncertain. "Maybe after she's had her way with them and they start to bore her, she returns them to the swamp? Just not in the way they'd hoped."

"So what are you saying? She's a horny old toad?" Beth couldn't stifle the erupting snicker. But she noticed her aunt didn't laugh. Didn't even crack a smile. To the contrary, she sat stone-faced, and the cocked eyebrow not a good sign. "What? I was kidding. You don't seriously believe some horny-ass old witch in the swamp was stealing men and turning them into toads, do you?"

Beth realized what she'd questioned. How did she doubt anything supernatural after what she'd witnessed firsthand with Moss? He'd turned into some sort of a reptilian type of creature right before her eyes, and she was going to doubt the plausibility of a witch turning virile men into toads? Her mind drifted back to Moss, and the image alone had her nipples puckering to tight, sensitive nubs as a slow warmth pooled in her center. Well, hell, Beth supposed she could understand the draw of anyone wanting to keep Moss all to themselves. Especially if that someone was a supposed conniving, horn dog old witch.

"You originally said you suspected who he was, yet when you started the story you said his name was never mentioned. What did you mean?" Beth asked, remembering her aunt's choice of words.

"You always were quick." Grace beamed. "And yes, you are correct," she continued. "As far as the legend goes, no name has ever been applied to the fearless young leader. However, local historical archives list one Mr. William Francis Markley as unaccounted for in the records of one Mrs. William Francis Markley. Only a note referencing the death of her husband turned up. No records reflect a Mr. Markley settling here. But there are a few vague mentions of the young Mrs. Markley, keyword being the Mrs., not widowed, but Mrs. Markley being added to towns register and church records. A few years later, another brief note declaring her husband, Mr. Markley, as deceased. Back in those days, all records would detail the husband's assets and possessions, limiting a wife's access. Understand that the rules were much different back then on what women could own without the aid of a husband. By all accounts, the only Markley mentioned with purchases, including the purchase of a piece of land, was a Mrs. Markley. Consider for a moment—if no Mr. Markley was around, why a death notice so many years later?"

Beth rolled the information around her mind a bit. It would make sense his widow would need to stay a Mrs. in order to retain the respect needed for making substantial purchases. The laws may have changed, or maybe rumor had it wrong and she'd fallen in love with someone else, thus declaring her husband dead.

"But as much as this does make sense, given the era when women had little to no rights, what makes you so certain this mysterious Mr. Markley is my Bog Man, or even the young leader who disappeared?"

"I don't think I know. That's who he is. I've seen him in my visions before."

"You've had visions of him?" Beth hadn't seen that coming.

"Sort of. Vague ones, mainly of his emotions and inner torments, and not just his. Sadly, others as well. Though his emotions have come through the strongest. Even after all these years, he's never forgiven himself for drinking too much and losing the children and his wife."

"But he didn't lose the children. You said they returned the next morning."

"And so they did. But, sweetie, he never returned. Therefore, he has no idea the children were all returned unharmed. To his knowledge, due to his indiscretion with alcohol, he not only lost the children but also lost his young bride. His pain and anguish have reached me many, many a night."

A sudden ache stabbed her heart. She now understood why Moss had walked away. He feared hurting her, or worse, losing her—too great a risk in his mind's eye. Hell, he still believed he'd lost his wife and the children and been the cause of their deaths. No wonder he seemed so confused and hurt. Technically, he was the one lost in the swamp, never making it out.

She had to find him. Prove the children as well as his wife had walked out of the swamp unscathed. Show how their lives had gone on, and how only his hadn't. No one had died on his watch or while under his care, and he needed to stop blaming himself for something that had never happened in the first place.

"Okay, what can you tell me about this supposed man-stealing witch causing all this bullshit?"

"She is quite old, strong, and extremely vengeful. Legend speaks of a sultry she-demon named Octavia. If the rumors are true, she isn't one to challenge lightly."

"Okay, warning taken. Now tell me how I find the ole hag and stop her."

"Very carefully, honey, and most certainly not on your own. We will have to plan carefully before making any moves toward her."

Chapter Eleven

Beth began her trip home, going over and over all the things she'd learned and tried to formulate the best plan. Should she find Moss and attempt to convince him of the truth first, or remove the threat itself first—the threat being the witch. Millions of questions and possibilities began running rampant in her thoughts.

She wasn't sure of anything except her desire to help Moss and experience his passionate touch again. She needed to make right that which had been made so terribly wrong. But how? Where should she start?

Lost in thought, she rounded one of the many sharp bends in the dirt road leading away from Grace's place. She was way out in the heart of the bayou when her sixth sense kicked in. A strong sensation of wrongness enveloped her. So intense, nausea had her stomach bubbling and her vision swimming. The lightheadedness too severe to continue driving, she attempted to brake and pull over. Smashed the pedal over and over with no reaction. The car, if anything, seemed to be speeding up. Panic assailed her mere seconds ahead of the sudden impact. She was in trouble, big trouble.

Her car plunged nose first into the swamp. She had a fleeting thought about the airbag recall notice she'd received and ignored before her skull careened with a jarring impact into the steering wheel. The incredible pain so shattering, tendrils wrapped around her entire body. Vibrating through each muscle and every bone. She was struggling to overcome the intense pain when the sounds of gushing water pierced her consciousness, but she couldn't breathe, much less think about escaping. The darkness enveloped her in a pain-free embrace.

Swamp Magic

Beth came to when the warm, murky swamp waters rose past her neck. She knew panicking wouldn't help, but damned if she didn't anyway. She was trapped in her car, in pain, and about to drown in what would no doubt end up being her watery coffin.

She freaked the hell out, screaming like a banshee as she lashed out toward the windshield before turning her frantic measures toward the driver's window. If she ever got out of this, she was never buying a car with electric windows again.

Her life began flashing before her eyes as she thought about all she'd wanted to do. Things she'd done and wanted to do again, like being in Moss's arms, wrapped entirely in hard, male love.

Luckily, before she began swallowing the not-so-appealing, thick, pea-green swamp water, a strange inner calm settled and brought with it an inner strength. She knew then she would not just sit there and die. Fuck that. If she was going out, then she would at least go out fighting. Okay, and maybe with a bit of screaming and cursing too.

Following her instincts, she started kicking on her door. Now that the car had fully submerged, the pressures should have equalized, making the door a more feasible route. She made a vow to never again tease Robby about watching all those "Survivor Man" type shows. She also vowed to pay more attention to them when they were on.

Seconds before running out of air, the strange sensation surrounding her grew stronger and with one last shove, the door opened with more velocity she would have thought possible. Shooting out of the car, she swam to the surface, gulping in the blessed swamp air. Never had humidity tasted as good as it did now.

She only had a few minutes of profound relief before thoughts turned to what might be lurking in the water with her. The soundtrack to *Jaws* began playing in her mind, and every nearby splash had her life flashing before her eyes again. Best she get on land fast.

Dragging her trembling body up onto the closest bank, she clawed her way farther from the water's edge. Gritty dirt embedded painfully deep under her nails as she distanced herself from the water's edge and any hungry gators lying in wait. She lay there trying to gather her thoughts and wits about her, her breath still coming in short, ragged bursts. She'd defeated death, but just barely, and was smart enough to know it.

*

"Did you really think you could do something like that and I'd just let you walk away?" The question dripped evil. Its hiss rolled through the swamp, causing a menacing echo. Though he couldn't see her, he felt her anger rumbling in her words.

If Moss had hackles, they would surely have raised. Instead he had scales—or, rather, *sometimes* had scales. Even so, he couldn't quite stop the slow, rising smirk he knew he sported as he remembered the humiliated state he'd left the bitch left in. Especially the knowledge that the incident had been all the old hag's fault. Once her spell wore off, clarity had kicked in, along with the thankful realization it hadn't been his Beth he'd been so brutal with, but the evil bitch herself.

How many others shared his fate? Were there only a few, or were there hundreds of others like him? Held captive for her own perverse sexual pleasures? After all this time, surely he would have encountered more than just Damien, the only other one like him he'd ever encountered, if there were.

A bright orb appeared and without warning burst into a bright, blinding flare. When his nocturnal sight adjusted to the sudden intrusion, Octavia stood before him, and she wasn't a happy camper.

"Well, smile while you can, my love, for it will be short-lived. I've left you a gift in the southeastern end of Bog's End. One I'm sure you'll enjoy." With her parting shot, she vanished. Simply vanished, in what appeared to be a puff of red smoke.

Her whispered promise oozed revenge, and he knew without a doubt she'd killed yet another innocent to prolong her worthless, miserable life. She loved nothing more than to flaunt her powers and, more to the point, her power of immortality. For that alone kept him bound to her, never to be free to go on to his family and beg their forgiveness. If he could even gain entrance into heaven. He knew, for the crimes he'd committed, he shouldn't be. No honorable or worthy man should even think to ask forgiveness for such a heinous crime as forsaking one's own wife for the lust of another. He hadn't meant to follow the devious Octavia that night. But when he'd caught sight of the beautiful woman, wandering about when looking for the children, he'd assumed the woman lost herself. But the way she'd toyed with him. Luring him, flirting as she had…he'd become enchanted and lost track of time. Didn't matter he'd been ensnared by a spell, he should have never followed in the first place.

A roar soared past his lips as hate, anger, and regret seethed from within at the very prospect of having to obey her command. After what he'd done to her, through no fault of his own, he knew what waited would be bad. He would be punished for acting out, though it had been her spell that caused it. Worse, he would not reap the physical end of her torture. No—instead she would force him to bear witness to her destruction of someone else.

Chapter Twelve

Beth came to with a pounding headache and no real recollection of anything short of the vague memory of a crash and dragging herself out of the swamp.

What the hell had she missed, between sighing in relief on the muddy bank she'd crawled onto and now? Peering downward, she realized she lay on a cold, wooden floor clad only in her underthings and an over-sized T-shirt. Her hands and arms were bound above her head to something resembling a wrought iron towel hook. She would have screamed her anger, frustration, and pain, but damned hellfire, she'd been gagged. Her tongue stuck to the roof of her mouth. She fought the panicked urge to begin gulping in air. Figured if she did while gagged, she'd hyperventilate—the last thing she needed to add to her *oh, shit,* list right about now.

Right then the she-devil came into view, starting from the bottom of a shimmery black silken train to wind upwards to a shapely yet slim pair of hips. Beth craned her neck to look farther, her gaze skimming past tits to the face of pure evil.

If not for the stone-cold look in the dark abyss of her eyes, Beth would have proclaimed her beautiful, exquisite even. Kind of like one of those fine porcelain dolls. Pretty, but damn well creepy as shit too.

But those eyes. You couldn't miss the evil lurking within them.

"So, you've awoken. Took you long enough. I would ask how you feel, but your dreadful appearance speaks for itself, and it's not as if you're able to answer me, anyway." The bitch shrugged as if Beth were an afterthought and nothing else. Her voice sounded like a cross between a purr and a hiss, with far more emphasis on the *hiss*.

"Damien, come to me," she cooed in a singsong voice that seemed to get caught in the gentle swamp winds and carry on and on. The type of sound so irritating you wanted to claw your ears out.

Beth no longer had any doubts about what she should do first. Taking out the witch became her first objective, since finding the bitch was no longer an issue. That made explaining the truth of the past to Moss secondary—after she found him, of course.

"I can't begin to understand his attraction to you. You look like a normal, boring little mortal female to me. And not even an attractive mortal. I would have thought him to have better taste than this."

Beth narrowed her eyes and thrust her chin out in defiance. The bitch damn well wouldn't get any begging from her, she fumed. Had she not been gagged, she would have spat back that she might not be as glamorous, but at least she was still young enough to count as warm blooded, unlike the bitch before her. Octavia might appear stunningly beautiful, but it was a false illusion no doubt thanks to some mirroring spell. *If not for her magic, I bet she'd pay a fortune in cosmetic surgery.* If the stories Grace told were true, the old bat ought to be mummified by now.

Moments later, the squeaking of a screen door followed by some big, heavy-sounding footsteps announced the arrival of the man the witch had called. Beth assumed it was Damien, whoever or whatever he turned out to be.

The wicked bitch of the south laughed almost flirtatiously as she sashayed into another room. Beth heard whispering, then two distinctive sets of steps heading back in her direction. An uneasy feeling settled in the pit of Beth's stomach, and she again tested her bindings. Nope, no wiggle room whatsoever. Shit, still stuck like Chuck.

"I know you're used to much prettier playthings, but I do hope you can make an exception with this one," the hag purred, nodding toward the heavy footsteps behind her. "You should be aware it will take about thirty more minutes for the spell to take hold."

"I think I'll manage fine," a deep, husky voice answered with a not-so-humorous edge.

Then the Damien dude Octavia mentioned came into view. Bad guy or not, and though she wouldn't have believed her reaction possible, her mouth went slack at the view of Mr. Heavy Footsteps. Maybe not as hot as Moss, but damn well nothing to sneeze at either.

He was at least six feet four inches and 250 pounds, and built to match his large frame. Monster pecs and ripped abs were visible through his half-unbuttoned shirt. Long, masculine legs bulged beneath tight faded jeans and…

Oh, shit.

Another muscle bulged too. Her gaze reached his face and she noticed he was more than aware where her gaze had landed. Heat bloomed in her cheeks.

His eyes were the coolest shade of blue she'd ever seen and popped in contrast against his black, shoulder-length hair. A firm, square jaw added to the rest of his almost obscenely handsome features. In other circumstances, and pre-Moss, she'd be drooling.

He smiled, but not in any form of hello. His eyes grew hooded, and he nodded in her direction.

"Here, or shall I take her back to my place?" Though he asked for permission, his tone commanded. He wanted her alone; of this Beth had no doubts. She also wondered what Octavia meant by a spell needing more time. As far as she could remember, she hadn't taken or been given anything. She hoped.

"While I will relish seeing her suffer, I have no doubts Moss is on his way here. I implied you had her already so he would search elsewhere. By now he must be aware of my ruse. Take her to your secret place do anything you wish, except kill her. I want Moss to witness her torture, and I'm not quite ready for her death yet."

Beth caught her cold stare and refused to show fear.

"As you wish, Octavia." Damien's gaze lazily scanned her from head to toe and back once more. It grew lustful and heated with each pass, leaving no question as to what he planned as soon as they made it to his place.

Octavia. Good, now she knew the old bitch's real name. Beth bookmarked the information for future use.

Octavia's attention once again returned to Beth. She sashayed over, her gown making a funny little rustling sound as it passed over the wooden planked floor. The witch knelt before her, leaning to place her face much too close for Beth's liking, and began whispering something too low for Beth to make out. A strange, hazy sensation crept through Beth. An odd, sleepy, lethargic state forced Beth to close her eyes against her own wishes. Everything around her grew heavy, and though she remained conscious of her surroundings, her eyes remained shut, and she had no energy to fight off the obvious spell.

Awareness skittered through her of being unbound and un-gagged by Damien. Though unable to see, she sensed a distinct male scent. Much to her surprise, he rather gently hoisted her over his shoulder and headed out away from the witch's cabin. The one time she was able to crack her eyes open, the swamp's waters shimmered just beneath her head. She also became semi-conscious of how her breasts bounced against Damien's back with each fierce step he took. He wasn't unaffected by this; each time they pressed into him, his breath hitched.

If nothing else, she knew one damn thing. This whole riding tossed over one's shoulder, sucked, and this made twice in as a little as two weeks.

A short time later, they entered what looked to be a cave, even upside down and under a weird spell. A few more steps into the mouth, and she noted all the intricate tunnels.

Oh, fucking perfect. Like she stood a shot in hell of remembering which tunnels he went down in this fuzzy ass state. But she'd have to try, if she hoped to ever find her way out. If she could escape past this rock of a man called Damien.

Damn Octavia and her stupid spell. Lucky for Beth, either she was stronger than the bitch thought, or the spell had been weakly cast. Though she wasn't knocked out, paying attention to the small details that might help her escape was almost impossible.

After what seemed a millennium, they entered an illuminated chamber. All around them candles flickered, and an image from *Phantom of the Opera* came to mind.

Damien eased her off the nice, firm, huge, muscled shoulder she'd started getting used to and laid her across his bed. Silent, he stood back and eyed her again. She shivered as he stared at her as if she were the main course at an all-you-can-eat buffet. His gaze implied he wondered where to start his feast.

"Take a picture—it lasts longer, asshat," she spat with as much venom as her cottonmouth could muster.

"My, what a smart mouth we have. A very pretty one, though, which I'm sure we could find a better use for." He didn't crudely grab himself, but instead subtly lowered his hand to his crotch.

Message received, loud and clear.

Beth narrowed her eyes in an attempt to keep from staring back with the telltale signs of the heat building within her. Damien's image before her wavered, flickering…until Moss stood before her.

Moss flat-out defined sexy. She started to wonder just what kind of spell the witch had cast. She didn't think her reactions were normal. Undiluted love for someone one minute. The next, unmistakable lust for someone else. Wait, no. Moss was here, and the longer she stayed near him, the more irresistible he became.

Though slow-simmering, her body began to tingle in low places in acute awareness of the boiling sexual tension permeating the cave. What frightened her most was how rapidly it flared. He even smelled good. Totally edible. She worried she'd start drooling at any minute, or worse, get up and go over to try to nibble on him. On one of those rippled muscles of his. One in particular. Moss matched her hungry gaze, proving he'd become aware of her aroused state. His confidence seemed rather like he'd been expecting her change of attitude. Why would she have not wanted to make love with Moss?

Her breathing became ragged as he stalked her way, brows arched, eyes positively gleaming, and cock swelling more with each heavy step.

She knew she should be scared or repulsed. No. No she shouldn't. This was Moss. Knew she should scream "no" at the top of her lungs and gear up for battle. She loved someone else. *No.* She did love someone, right? Yes, she loved Moss. Wait. Confusion took her to unthinkable places as she shook her head, trying to regain her previous thoughts.

Why did she hold back, when Moss clearly wanted her? Wasn't she in love with him? She could almost remember someone else, but then her mind grew clouded again as she strained to remember who. Memories vanished until only the here and now remained as the room spun around in mad fashion. The temperature became hot and humid, unbearable. Mugginess in the room caused an almost claustrophobic sense to envelope her. Drops of perspiration began beading across her skin, sliding down crevices here and there, and with each drop, Moss licked his lips.

"So hot…can't breathe." She shook, as if she burned from the inside out, and yanked at the smothering tee before jerking it off as Moss crawled up the enormous bed toward her. His direction caused her pulse to jump as his head dipped by her knee. A hot tongue licked the insides of first one, then the other of her slightly bent knees. Goose bumps raced across her flesh. She watched as if through someone else's eyes as his large, calloused hands firmly spread her legs farther apart.

His knees on the bed and hands on her thighs, he moved lower until his face hovered over her pussy and a finger pulled her thong to the side. He nipped the inside of her calf, and she heard a faint noise. Became aware the noise came from her. A sharp intake of breath combined with almost a purr. She purred? When the hell had she ever purred, and what the hell had she forgotten? The heat of his mouth taunted her, as did the sharp nips he gave. Did he want her to beg?

Then his tongue began lapping her as if she were an ice cream cone on a hot summer day. He showered her with oral love, and then he suddenly stopped. She glared at him even as she reached for him. He'd been in an awkward position, and in her confused and needy state of lust, she hadn't noticed. He shifted until his shoulders rested between her thighs. He gently pushed her into a more supine position, which left her head resting on the satin pillows scattered across his bed.

Giving her no pause to prepare, his mouth returned to the exploring assault on her lower body as one hand inched higher, taking its own explorative path, taking in every curve and indent her body had. She sighed. She was his and he was hers.

All her earlier reservations vanished. And for the life of her, she didn't even remember what they'd been. All she knew was Moss. Somehow his hands and tongue were everywhere at once, and damn, but the dude had talent.

She heard a low growl, and from the vibrations against her bare thighs, knew it came from him. Moss with that magical tongue of his. Her bra and her thong went flying, and his mouth found and suckled her clit. Instinct drove her hips upwards as the world she thought she knew came crashing down around her in one hell of an orgasmic ride.

Chapter Thirteen

"Damn you to hell. Where is she?" Moss spat as he stormed into the witch's sanctuary, slamming the rickety door hard enough it splintered into pieces.

"Where you will not find her, my love, or rather not find her in time," she cooed, sarcastic and cool.

"What did you do to her?" Moss seethed, barely keeping his rage in check. Even if killing her were possible, he wouldn't risk losing the only link to Beth.

"Oh, worry not, my love. She is, at this moment, perfectly fine and rather enjoying herself, I would suspect." She eyed him, though she was careful to keep him at arm's length, his desire to rip her throat out clear. Her gown rustled as she continued moving farther away. Subtly, but nonetheless moving into a safer position.

He knew her idea of enjoyment and those of others usually never agreed. The slick look she sported made his stomach turn, knowing it meant something sick and twisted.

"I demand you tell me what you've done." He braced his stance for an attack. Feet planted wide apart, hands curling into fists, yet resting at his side ready.

"Oh, you *demand* do you? Don't forget your true circumstance here. As a result of your recent actions, I decided you needed a firm reminder of where and what your exact place is here. So I arranged for a surprise. One that will undoubtedly clear up the sudden misperceptions you may have once and for all. Let us cut to the chase, shall we? You remember Damien, don't you?" Her cold smile chilled him to the core in fear of what may be happening to Beth. It infuriated him as well, with the knowledge he couldn't do anything. Yet.

"We've met," he admitted, remembering the only shifter he'd ever encountered. Apprehension settled deep as memories of the all-but-forgotten shifter resurfaced.

"Yes, I thought you might. I believe you met during one of Damien's more, shall we say, sentimental moments."

Sentimental? Was that what she called the slaying of an innocent man? Damien had no choice but to kill the poor sap, but Moss remembered the horror on his face at doing so. Moss and Damien both understood the man had thought he defended an innocent woman. No amount of explaining would change his mind over what he thought had transpired. Octavia had engineered the entire episode to teach Damien his place. She had conjured bruises to appear all over her body and told the man, who thought he was wooing and protecting the honor of a proper lady, that a foul man, namely Damien, had attempted to rape her.

The poor fool believed her every lie and attacked Damien full force. Even after Damien bested him and planned to release him, she appeared again, dropped her gown, whimpered, and showed even more faux bruises. These covering her inner thighs in the shapes of handprints. Her little feat worked all too well, enraging the man to such a state of frenzy he tried to kill Damien before Damien gained the upper hand again. This time, Damien knew he had no choice but to kill the man. There'd been no doubt the man would continue in his attacks. Nothing else could be done to prevent it from happening.

Damien hadn't wanted to kill him. He'd understood and sympathized with the man, whose only crime had been protecting a wronged woman, or so he'd believed.

"What about Damien?" Moss asked, knowing whatever she said wouldn't be pleasant.

"Well, it seems he, too, saw your little mortal woman wandering about in my swamps. I think he became rather smitten with her as well, though I can't understand what either of you find so attractive in anyone so simple. She seemed rather shaken, poor dear. Unfortunately for her, she crashed that little dented piece of metal she called a car. I sure hope she didn't suffer any head trauma."

"She is with him?" Moss asked, conflicted over the thought. Relief she was with someone like Damien who would keep her safe combated against her claim of Damien being smitten by Beth. He feared what changes Damien had undergone in these past years. Would he help her escape Octavia's clutches, or would his desire for a female overwhelm his once-human qualities?

"Oh, how delightful and refreshing. You're wondering about his intentions toward her? Well, let me make this clear. Unlike you, Damien has come to respect what I can do...and what I can offer. I chose to prove this again to him by offering the gift of a woman. Your human woman, who'd captured his interests. I've given him free rein to do with her as he so pleases. At least for now."

Images of the dark Damien seducing his Beth came to mind, images of Beth squirming under the beast as he forced himself upon her, pinning her under him, penetrating her. Moss roared in rage and stalked toward Octavia as the predator within clawed to get out.

Octavia threw her arm up, palm out. A familiar sensation hit, of concrete pouring through his veins, weighing him down. He fought against the heavy feeling so hard blood seeped from his nostrils. Pain exploded in his brain as her mental scolding for his outburst scoured each nerve.

"Now, settle yourself this instant. Do not make me hurt you anymore—but the decision is yours."

He stilled, dropping to one knee and shaking from the brutal mental attack. He knew becoming physically impaired wouldn't help free Beth from the witch's, or from Damien's clutches. He'd need to keep his temper in check, play his cards right in order to regain his freedom and rescue Beth from whatever fate Damien planned.

"Don't fret. She won't suffer extensively, as I do not intend to let her live for very long. I refuse to allow some simpleton who hasn't yet learned to mind their own damn business to run amok causing havoc in my swamps, now can I?"

"You will not touch a hair on her head." He wanted to strike. Take out the threat Octavia represented, but he refrained at the last moment.

"Please don't force me to hurt you again," she hissed ominously before holding her hand in front of his face and making a fist. The minute her hand clasped together, pain rocketed from his mind to his stomach, bringing him back to the floor.

"I have no intention of touching the filthy little bitch," she went on. "I'll even promise not to lift a finger to her." Her sudden, vicious laugh told Moss her promise meant nothing. "You see, I placed a unique spell upon her. At this very moment, or soon thereafter, she will believe she is with you. She will see Damien's image as yours. For good measure, I added a touch of lust to the mirroring spell. Oh, my. Can't you just visualize them now? All the delightful things Damien must be doing to her as we speak. All the things she herself is pleading for. I'd imagine she's begging for sexual relief about now. Oh, to be a bug on their wall right now." She laughed loudly, taunting him with graphic verbal images of his Beth with another male. Thoughts of the pleasures Damien would find with her pushed him over the edge, and before he could stop himself, he launched into Octavia.

"You fool," she hissed, sidestepping his attack by becoming more shadow than substance. "How dare you think to attack me? Have you forgotten, my dearest? To kill me, in fact, kills you too?"

Chapter Fourteen

"Oh—Moss—yes." Beth moaned. "You came back." She sounded so happy and relieved.

Damien bent his head in shame after Beth called him by another's name. Part of him—the small human part he'd managed to keep hidden from Octavia—wondered how he could take her and still live with himself. She only wanted him because she thought him to be Moss. The other shifter, whom it appeared she loved. Damien longed for the warmth and compassion of an innocent mortal woman. Even reminding himself she called for Moss didn't stem his desire for her.

Her body responded to his touch. Her legs spread, eager, as her hands reached between them to stroke him. Enticing him into entry as soft mewls escaped past lush lips. Gently he rocked forward between her legs until the heat and dampness of her core touched the broad head of his cock. He shuddered from his own need.

"Moss, Please don't stop. I need you…now. Need release," she begged in panting whispers.

Torn as his own needs and desires gripped him by the balls, he almost lost the fight. The extreme spell Octavia had cast wracked her body with frantic bouts of lust. It also caused a frighteningly high fever as Damien hovered over her in indecision. She would get worse unless he gave her release. He'd seen this spell in action before. Understood the gravity behind the physical and mental madness it unleashed. His engorged cock bobbed at her entrance; her eyes glowed with the ferocity of her need. She again arched upwards, her breasts skimming ever so close to his mouth.

He realized neither of them had a safe way out. He'd been set up, again, to be Octavia's hand of justice, and the dawning of this knowledge was painful. He didn't want to hurt the woman beneath him.

"Please," she whimpered. Her body, writhing in agony beneath him, took him to the brink of sanity. The pain of not fulfilling the spell took its toll upon her, the fever rising dangerously high. Once a spell this potent had been cast, there would be serious consequences if its demands were not met quickly.

No matter what he did, he'd be damned either way. If he took her while she thought him to be another, it would damn well be near rape in his book. If he didn't, she would suffer in excruciating pain and quite possibly die.

His mind set and resolve firm, he prepared to do what needed to be done. He would rather Beth hate him than die in agony. Yet even though he did what he needed to ensure her survival, and would forever be plagued by guilt, he would enjoy every second of being with her.

Her scent was so unique and compelling. It stirred old emotions in him he'd thought long-since dead. Her body molded against his to form a perfect fit. Beckoning him to touch, lick, and savor it.

Her hands captured the sides of his face and brought his mouth to hers.

All time for rational thought had evaporated. They were each far beyond reproach, and now moving under the compulsion of the spell.

His tongue entered heaven to mingle with hers and, God help him, but her taste brought out the wild in him as he lined himself up with her wet, ready entrance. She cried out and scored his back with her nails as the spell continued to ravage her mind and body. She shook beneath him, tossed her head back and forth, gasping for air and fulfillment. Her vibrations and her squirming only heightened his own sense of need.

"Forgive me," he whispered before seating himself within her in one swift, filling stroke.

His reward came when her hips lunged off the bed to meet him and, for a second, he feared he'd hurt her. Her entrance was tight, and her little body seemed to struggle to accommodate the sudden intrusion. Her little gasps sounded as though pain and torment had been vanquished and replaced with ecstasy, easing his mind.

With each quick, deep stroke, she kneaded his ass and pulled him closer. The fact he aided in easing the pains of her spell, coupled with bringing her pleasure, more than stoked him. Her hearty responses continued to act as an aphrodisiac as all the blood in his body rushed to one location. His cock was so damn hard; entering her warm, tight sheath had been exhilarating.

Her sexy sounds drove him crazy as she bucked, arched, grasped and sighed. Her sexual frenzy added to his own pleasures as he continued pounding into her. A fire raged within as he fought off his need for release. He wanted to stay with his angel as long as possible, and once she achieved release, the spell might break.

"Oh, Moss, I've needed you so."

"And I you." He might not be Moss, but he didn't doubt Moss missed her. He drove deep and her legs locked around his waist. Their combined sweat began acting as natural lubricant, and their skin slid back and forth across each other. The resulting friction pebbled her nipples to utter perfection as they jabbed his chest, begging for some serious attention.

Far be it from him to remain ignorant.

Damien leaned over and suckled one into his mouth. The pearl bloomed even more as he rolled the bud around his mouth, gently nipping between each pass of his amply skilled tongue.

Her fingers tangled in his hair as she pressed his mouth against her breast, attempting to coax him into continuing his oral administrations—like he needed any encouragement. He chuckled at her aggressive bedroom nature and wondered how much came from the spell and how much of her behavior was truly her.

Had she shown Moss, whom she called for, this side? Or had Damien brought out the hellcat within her? His touch, his special attentions, and his own unique scent? Could he ever hope such a thing possible?

Deep down, Damien suspected the spell. But maybe the magic opened a dormant doorway for her, allowing her to be free of any and all sexual limitations she may have placed upon herself. He hoped maybe a small part was a direct reaction to being with him.

It had been so long since he'd had this kind of unity with anyone, much less such a young, vibrant woman as Beth. What he wouldn't give to hear her crying out *his* name when he made her come instead of Moss's. To listen to her sultry voice uttering his name through her kiss-swollen lips. A pipe dream he'd pray for each night, as she loved and longed for another even as he slid languidly into her. He prayed for her benefit she wouldn't remember their union tomorrow, or at the very least would somehow understand the necessity of his actions. He'd had no choice but to reciprocate her sexual advances even though he'd known she thought him to be her beloved Moss.

Even as his body tensed, prepping for its release, he cursed Octavia to all damnation. Prayed one day he could find redemption and escape from her all-powerful hold on him.

He grabbed Beth's knees in a bruising grip, holding her wide open as he rode the building crest to a fevered release. Heard her breathing become hitched, erratic, and he scented she rode the cusp, herself. And with one last, near-violent thrust, the crest broke and they rode the wave of release together. Her cries of ecstasy mingled with his own rumbling roar. He relished watching her lids flutter open and the euphoric expression of release glimmer in her eyes before confusion and horror replaced any semblance of peace.

Her physical withdrawal hurt less than the betrayed look she wore now. "Who…who the hell are you?" she asked, angry yet tearing up all the same.

Damien sat back on his haunches, wanting to reach out and console her. Take away her pain and fear. "My name is Damien. How much do you remember of your past day?" He didn't want to add to her confusion, but needed to know if she remembered Octavia or even the spell.

"I, uh, don't remember much, actually. Everything's all fuzzy, like I've been on a week-long drunk or something," she replied, scooting farther up in the bed.

Sympathetic, yeah, of course he was. She awoke in a stranger's lair and he could only imagine her level of discomfort. But seeing her turn pale in bewilderment and anguish at being in his bed and in his arms hurt, though, he'd feared this ending.

"Do you remember a witch named Octavia?"

She pulled the sheet up to her chin as she slowly tried to scoot away, closer to the headboard and farther from him. He stood, pulling on some loose sweats to help ease her discomfort at his naked state. He watched her eye him warily, not dropping her gaze from his. He saw a light go off, a small something jarred from her spell-laden memory.

"I…yes. I was driving…and then darkness surrounded me and she showed up. I was supposed to do something. Find somebody, I think?"

He caught himself from reaching out to tuck an errant strand of her silken hair behind her ear. Wanted to see her face and those gorgeous eyes peer at him with lust instead of fear. Instead, he stayed frozen in place as she ran a hand through her hair, pulling it up and away from her face, as she appeared to struggle to remember what she'd forgotten. She glared at him with accusation.

"How did I come to—to be here with you, like, uh…this?" she asked, still clutching the sheet around her for dear life.

"A spell was cast upon you. One that required specific actions for the effects to be neutralized."

"A spell, as in magic? Like hocus pocus and abracadabra and all that jazz?"

He watched as she chewed her bottom lip, deep in thought, trying, no doubt, to come to grips with his statement.

"What kind of spell was placed on me?" she pushed, growing more agitated than frightened now.

"Apparently she placed some kind of sexual spell on you. One that left you writhing in pain and fevered from lack of sexual release."

He wouldn't tell her, but her face turned the cutest shade of red.

"What did I do?" Cringing, she peered back at him.

He schooled his expression to give away nothing as he tried to formulate an answer that would protect her from any embarrassment. "Pain had overcome you and—"

"Oh, so then you—uh—we...oh, God."

Shame washed through him, compelling him to turn away. He realized a true gentleman would have already offered her some warm, heavy clothes. He didn't question she'd feel exposed and vulnerable, naked and in a stranger's bed. Not to mention caves weren't known for their warmth.

"I guess I should thank you, for um...well." She shrugged, seeming at a loss for words. "But I'm still not clear how exactly I came to be here, or with you."

"I'm at Octavia's, the witch who cast the spell upon you, command. She called me forth and gave me orders to bring you here. I swear to you I was unaware of the exact spell she placed. She said she'd placed one, but until we arrived here you were still unconscious and not..." He broke off, unsure how to describe her condition without furthering her agitated state. "It wasn't until later I discovered what kind of spell she'd cast."

She looked off then, as if she continued to struggle for even one memory. Fighting to remember who she'd been out looking for. The memories were there, locked away deep down. Time would release them but the wait would be torturous.

"Fuck." She jerked back in the bed, anger radiating from each movement.

"Frustrating, I'm sure." He readily admitted.

"Um, no offense, but a wee more than just frustrating. It's like, well..."

Damien's gut twisted at her obvious distress. He had nothing against Moss, but for a few fleeting minutes, he... Well. It was pointless to even ponder such thoughts. She wasn't his and never would be. Unless...

"Here, put this on," Damien offered, handing her one of his T-shirts, knowing it would hit her at dress length. I think you will find yourself more at ease, and if nothing else, warmer. I admit the place can get rather damp and chilly," he stated, gazing about the cavern he called home.

"Where is here exactly?"

"My chambers," he rumbled with pride.

*

Essentially, he'd told her squat. His chambers. Where in the hell was that, and why did it seem like they were in a cave? And why did her mind scream she'd forgotten something serious? A nagging reminder she'd been on an important mission. Geez, but her head throbbed. Each pulse felt like someone cracking her over the head.

"Moss," she squealed, as if she'd just found the long-missing piece of a jigsaw puzzle.

She yelled it so suddenly, Damien turned back toward her before she had a chance to pull the shirt he'd given her the rest of the way down. Her breasts swayed a bit, and the look he gave her told her that, though he might have had no choice in doing the deed with her, he'd more than enjoyed himself.

"I don't blame you, you know," she whispered, surprising Damien as well as herself.

"Maybe you should." He turned away, his head hung low.

She sat on the edge of the bed and wondered if Moss would understand what had happened. Infidelity? Could one, under a spell of this kind, still be held accountable? Would he understand what had happened and still believe in her? Still want her? Hell, that was if she even found him.

"This Moss, he loves you?" Damien asked quietly, not ready to admit yet he knew the reptile shifter.

"Uh, well…I'm really not sure how to explain. It's kind of complicated."

"What's complicated about loving a woman like you?" he asked, still refusing to meet her eyes.

She wasn't sure what he meant by "a woman like her," but he'd made it sound like he thought her honorable or something. She couldn't quite put her finger on exactly what he aimed for.

"Well, this witch of yours, Octavia, led him to believe a lie. Shit! I remember now." When Damien remained silent, she continued. "She told him a huge, horrible lie, and I was trying to find him to tell him the truth."

The heavy wooden door to the chamber's entrance slammed open so hard that when it made contact with the cave wall it splintered into a thousand tiny shards. Instinctively, she jumped, lunging toward Damien, who'd come to place himself between her and the door in a protective stance.

"Step away from her," a very angry, predatory hiss demanded.

His hair hung loose and wet, his bare chest heaving and glistening with sweat. He appeared as though he'd gone on a rampage through the swamp. He trembled with rage. But it was the glowing green eyes that tipped her off to the instability of the seething man before her.

"Moss?"

Chapter Fifteen

Moss stormed into the candlelit chamber and stilled as he seemed to scent something in the air. His eyes took on an ominous glare before he turned to stalk toward Damien. His intentions were clear, the resounding threat of violence present in each precise step.

Beth watched in horror as Damien switched from defensive to offensive. His muscles bunching, teeth bared, as he met Moss's deathly glare with an equally lethal look. They began a slow, macabre dance, circling as each took on more predatory features.

"You have been with him." A statement—gruff, accusing, menacing—not a question.

"It is not what you think, *Bog Man*," Damien stated with a bit too much emphasis on "Bog Man." It was a clear jab at who Moss was, who he resented being.

Beth never saw who struck first. She only caught a blur and a whistling of air before Damien went from standing in front of her to fighting for his life sprawled across the floor. She knew she'd never forget the grotesque sound of bones cracking or watching skin splitting, spilling blood onto the cave's stone floor.

"Stop it!" she screamed so loud she swore she burst a lung. But it wasn't loud enough, as neither so much as paused.

Fists continued to fly, as did muffled thuds as enormous knuckles made contact with flesh. Praying neither would be left with permanent injuries, she tried to figure out a way to make the meatheads stop.

Adrenaline and testosterone permeated the room. She shook like a leaf at what she feared would be the death of one of the two men she cared about. She didn't want them fighting, especially not over her, and if she planned to stop them it had to be now. Bloody pools already sat coagulating in crevices about the floor. Going by the sounds of their grunts, neither was ready to concede the fight.

She called upon her secret gift. The one that set her apart from the rest of her other female kin. She went into Moss's mind first, showering him with images of the witch casting the lust spell on her. Next she shot into Damien's, grabbed the images of his heartfelt apology for having no choice but to have fucked her, and literally transferred them into Moss's mind, praying he'd see and understand the situation for what was.

Both men stilled at her initial telepathic intrusions. Stilled even while gripping the other fiercely for dominance. Neither trusted the other's momentary pause in battle, but they stopped nonetheless. Once all images had been transferred back and forth, she waited for them to process what they'd seen. Moments later, they backed away from each other and stood, hesitant. Each eyed the other warily, but they were no longer swinging at each other.

Whew, much better. At least it was a start. "He didn't have a choice, Moss. Neither did I," she explained, hoping to not rekindle the anger she'd just extinguished.

Still breathing heavily, and appearing torn with raw emotion, Moss said nothing. The pained look he wore tore her heart in two and brought tears to her eyes. She wasn't sure what else to say. How else could she explain what had transpired between her and Damien. A bit calmer but still taut, ready for another assault, Damien attempted a better explanation.

"You of all people should understand what the cold bitch is capable of. You know once she has cast a spell, there is no turning back. Would you have preferred me to leave her in agonizing pain? Preferred me to risk her dying by the fever? She was in excruciating pain, and the fever was high enough I chose not to risk her life."

"I would have preferred you not to have fucked her. Preferred you to have located me. I would have helped ease her suffering."

Oh, shit. Beth knew Moss still seethed in anger. Though she did pick up confusion as well. Also that he felt betrayed. By both of them. Yet for now, they had him at least listening.

"So you wish for me to have taken the time to search for you? Hunt you for God only knows how long out in the swamps, all while she screamed in agony?" Damien's eyes narrowed angrily as he took in Moss's pause for consideration. "You care so little for her, Bog Man, that you would have chosen that for her? Answer carefully, for the way you answer will play a large part in how I intend to go forth."

"Is that a threat, Road Kill?" Moss snickered.

Road Kill? What in the hell was Moss insinuating? Moss's ploy to bait Damien had worked. Damien's eyes narrowed as he bristled at Moss's name-calling. His formerly defensive stance switched to a decidedly offensive one. The last thing anyone needed was for them to throw down again. She thought she should jump between them to settle them down, but instead, she froze. She needed to hear Moss's answer, from his lips. Moss's labored breaths boomed through the room, yet he refused to speak or even look her way. Her heart broke into a million tiny pieces.

"Your lack of answer is enough for me," she said. "I judged you wrong, Moss, and I apologize for placing too much responsibility on you concerning me. Damien, I understand what you did and why, and please believe I hold no ill will toward you. I thank you for having cared enough, even though you didn't really know me, to not want me left in agony or worse."

She watched, angry and bitter as Damien, who seemed to care more about her, a mere stranger, than her own Bog Man did, lowered his head in acknowledgement of her words. Head held high, she turned to flee before the as of yet unshed tears poured free. When she got to the chamber's entrance, she turned to face Moss one last time. She would do what she'd set out to do. It seemed only fitting.

"Moss, regardless of what transpired between us, you have a right to know the truth." She used her nails to score her palms to battle back the tears. The sting worked for the moment. "You were not responsible for your wife's death or that of the children."

His head whipped toward her as shock replaced the angry look on his face. "What did you just say?" A mere whisper, yet pain rode loud in each syllable, and his face contorted in sheer torture.

"You killed no one that night. It was you she zeroed in on, not your wife or the children. Their lives went on. Yours was the only one to have ended that night."

"How can that be true? I searched all night for them. Kept searching until she convinced me of their deaths." Moss dropped his head into his hands. Beth sensed how badly he wanted to believe the words she spoke. How much he needed to, but he feared letting go of the long-held obligation of guilt. Hell, he probably didn't even know how to after all this time.

"Records in the courthouse prove their existence. Proof they went on to live full lives, and settled happily in this town. What I speak is the truth, and you needed—no, *deserved* to know."

With those words, she turned on her heel and left, taking with her what little dignity she had left, though it felt more like it dragged along the floor behind her. Her heart hurt, her mind was muddled, and she just wanted to go home, cry, and curl up for a week. Sure, none of this shit had been her fault, but she understood what it must look like from his side. That still didn't change the fact he'd acted like a grade-A pompous ass.

She hadn't gone far when a faint scuffling sound began, and Damien's voice called out for her. Mortification kicked in and she bolted. Ran from having to deal with any more accusations or confrontations. Ran from the man she thought she'd shared something phenomenal and different with.

Ran from everything she'd left back in that room. She couldn't handle any more drama right now. It had all been too much, too fast.

Hell, she didn't even know where she was running to; she just knew she wanted out of this damn cave and the hell away from both of the biggest male egos she'd ever met. So onward she continued, not caring how lost she might become. Anything would be better than having to face off with either of them again.

She rounded a corner so fast she didn't realize there were no torches lighting this path, and before she could put the brakes on, she felt the ground disappear from beneath her feet. The strange, weightless feeling of falling kicked in. Day became night as she blindly reached outwards, clawing for anything she could grasp, and thankfully semi-landed on a shelf of sorts. She was afraid to move for fear she would fall again. She couldn't see what she was on, or how big it was, and didn't have any time to think about it before it crumbled beneath her in a scattering of loose rock and dirt.

She screamed in terror and heard a strange cracking just before the many brilliantly bright stars swarmed her vision and she fell into mental oblivion.

Chapter Sixteen

"You're a fool, Moss. Beth was a victim of Octavia's temper, and you damn well know it," Damien hissed.

"What do *you* know about love? You've what? Loved the she-bitch for how long now and expect me to believe you got played?" Moss answered as rage bubbled forth. His fangs extended, and the scaled tattoos spread—a sure indication he anticipated launching into another physical altercation with his old acquaintance.

"You should understand more than anyone exactly how evil she is, my friend. I was young and stupid many a year ago. Much like you were, on the ill-fated night she found you. Oh, yeah, Moss. I know your story. Heard the tale of how she lured you farther and farther into the twisted swamps. I also get you followed her for reasons far from noble in nature." Damien's eyes had taken on a lethal glow, one that indicated he, too, still considered their brawl far from over.

"Whatever happened is none of your concern," Moss spat, lunging forward, wanting nothing more than to rip Damien's throat out.

"Hit a sore spot, did I?" Damien goaded, sidestepping Moss's attack with ease. "Nothing pisses me off more than someone who had something special and was too stupid to know it. If you're not going after her, I will. I did my duty, told you the truth, and if your head is too far up your Neanderthal ass, then so be it. Lucky me."

Moss froze as Damien's words sunk in.

"I can't help but wonder if Beth knows the whole truth of that night?" Damien questioned.

Moss considered his options. Beat the hell out of Damien, which at the very least would make him feel better, or find Beth and attempt to sort out everything that had happened. He opted for Beth, stalking out to find her before she got herself into any more trouble. Or before he killed Damien, wiping the cocky smirk off his face permanently. He sensed Damien following and didn't give a shit if the prick wanted to watch. Moss had every intention of finding Beth and carrying her the hell out of Damien's lair. If Damien didn't like it, Moss would deal with the cretin later. Beth belonged with him, and he had no intentions of sharing her with Damien or anyone else.

Now, he need only convince Beth of this.

They hadn't gone far when she screamed. He heard the terror in it, then the most horrid sounding thud. But the terrifying silence that followed was worst of all. Her scream stopped as if cut with a knife. It had simply quit when the thud had.

All animosities tossed aside, he and Damien dashed toward where the scream had originated. He'd never been more frightened in his life. Not when the witch had cursed him, not even when he thought he'd let his wife down, allowing her to become lost. Yes, he'd loved her, but theirs had been an arranged marriage. They'd grown up together, had been friends, and he'd done what he thought expected of him. He'd cared for her, yes. Loved her so hard he lost his breath? No.

He would not lose Beth.

*

Beth brushed her hand across her forehead and wondered what the strange, damp, sticky stuff was that seemed to be matted on it. Bewildered, she tried to sit, and as her hands went to the floor to push herself up, one hand couldn't seem to find the floor. She felt around and felt a rock ledge not far under her and only space beyond that.

She glanced over in that direction and saw nothing. The utter darkness she found herself cloaked in seemed endless, and she instinctively leaned right and breathed a sigh of relief when her body rubbed against the cool solidness of the rock wall next to her.

Carefully, she patted her hands all around her bottom half and found, within inches in front of, behind and to one side of her, nothing but air. That was when the true terror set in, and the vague image of falling into an endless abyss took hold and she plastered herself against the caves wall. She remembered the fall, the sharp crack and pain before oblivion stole her away. Where the hell had she ended up, and how in Hades would she get herself the hell out?

More memories inched back into her mind. Moss and Damien fighting, the hurt and betrayed expression etched on Moss's gorgeous face. Awakening in Damien's arms, quite naked. All those flooded back with a bitter vengeance.

"Oh, God, what have I done, and with whom?" she whispered through waves of shame and anxiety.

Damien had implied she'd been out of her mind with desire and carnal needs, but had she? Did some damn spell really cause her extreme reaction? She believed in magic. Had been around the essence of witchcraft all her life, but until Octavia, had never witnessed such strong, dark magic being practiced before.

Well, hell, of course dark magic had the ability to turn her into a stark raving nymphomaniac. She knew people toyed with that kind of power; she'd just never had a whammy of that sort placed on her. Oh, she'd heard rumors through the years. She'd read about the horrors of love spells gone awry; where either the spell had pushed the intended farther away, or brought them so close the caster of the spell couldn't move an inch without their so-called beloved. But being on the receiving end of a hardcore, X-rated, sexual spell? She'd never had reason to think about such a thing.

Either way, the episode with Damien had to have appeared bad from Moss's perspective. Truthfully, had she walked in on Moss with someone else—well, it wouldn't have ended with a pretty scene. She would have ripped a bitch a new face.

Damn old hag will wish she'd never met me by the time I'm done with her.

Oh, yeah, the bitch would pay for this. Not only had she fucked up Moss's life and most likely Damien's too, but now Octavia seemed intent on screwing Beth's over as well.

Well, fuck the old bag of bones. Beth didn't plan on lying down, pun intended, and taking it. She'd gather the aunts, and together they'd conjure up their own damn whammy. Yep, they'd fuck Octavia's world all up by sending the old hag back to whatever hell she'd spawned from. Well, as soon as Beth figured out how to get out of her current predicament.

"Beth." Her name rang out from far above her. Her heart thundered. Thank God they'd found her. She'd started to call back, until she froze in mid thought, her voice suddenly forsaking her.

She wanted to be saved, but being saved right now also meant another round of confrontation. She couldn't handle seeing the hurt again on either man's face. Nor was she truly ready to admit what she'd done. What she'd experienced with Damien. Yes, it might have only transpired due to a spell, but from what she remembered, she'd enjoyed his efforts at saving her.

Fuck that. She wasn't about to fall off into the freaking abyss just to save face.

"Down here," she managed to squeak. The current terror at her situation was evident in her quivering tone.

"We see you. Do *not*, I repeat, do *not* move one muscle," Moss ground out.

He sounded as scared as she did, and she was the one perched on the ledge next to a drop-off with no bottom in sight. She overheard the guys whispering above her.

"Even with my heightened sense of sight, I cannot make out the bottom."

"I can't either, Damien. We need to get to her fast."

"Beth, do what Moss said—don't move an inch."

"Uhh, like duhh," she spat, sore, tired and a little sarcastic.

"She seems a bit miffed," Damien muttered under his breath, apparently perplexed as to why. Typical male, she mused.

"Of course she would; she's been through tremendous events these last few days." Moss sounded rather defensive of her, winning another brownie point. Just hearing him get defensive on her behalf made her heart go pitter-pat. Maybe he hadn't been as angry as she'd originally thought. She could hope, couldn't she?

A light spattering of rocks and loose dirt came raining down, and try as she might, she wasn't able to hold back her startled shriek. She tried to shield her eyes from the falling debris while not falling over the edge in the process. Her bottom was way too close to the edge, though she hadn't moved anything but her arms.

"God, Beth, are you all right?" they both yelled, sounding frantic.

"Uh, yeah, but guys, whatever you did, please, please don't do it again." She tried to add a touch of humor to her voice, but knew she hadn't quite succeeded. The tumbling rocks had been a quick reminder of how potentially deadly her situation was.

"Look, we both can't go down to get her. Do you have any rope?" Moss asked taking charge.

"Yeah, hold on a sec. I've got some back in my chambers."

"What's going on up there? Is something wrong? What aren't you telling me?" She sure as hell hoped nothing else had gone wrong.

Please, no more surprises today. Please, please, please, She prayed.

"Beth, baby, hold still. Do not move a muscle until I can reach you, okay?" Moss called down to her.

"Exactly where do you think I would go, oh, Swampy One?" Okay, so her nerves were shot and she'd become a bit hysterical. So sue her. When Moss rumbled above her, chuckling at her clever yet smart-ass reply, something inside her instinctively calmed. As though her soul understood Moss would never allow her to get hurt. Well, not seriously anyway.

"Damien has gone to get rope, and as soon as he's back, I'm coming down to get you. Beth, I swear on my life, I'm not letting anything happen to you. I just need you to remain still and calm."

"Okay, I'll be here. I don't have any better place to be right now, though I am checking my calendar as we speak."

"Oh, I can think of many better places you could be," he teased.

"You can, can you?"

"Oh yes, I most certainly can." His voice dropped even deeper, becoming more baritone.

"And where would that be?" She had her suspicions, but as angry as he'd been, she wanted him to say it.

"I think you already know the answer to that. Don't you, Beth?"

"Moss?"

"Yeah?"

"I'm…I'm so very, very sorry." Her voice lowered, quivering as she uttered those painful but truthful words. The need to apologize overwhelmed her, and yet she feared her timing.

"I know, and we can discuss what took place later. Right now, though, let's concentrate on getting you to safety." Though his words spoke assurance, she couldn't mistake the pain lacing them.

Damien returned and, sensing the uneasy silence between them, wordlessly handed Moss the rope, taking in his old friend's unsure appearance.

Light shuffling began above her, and she knew Moss was gearing up to rappel down to her. Just as she began to sigh in relief, an evil laugh echoed through the cave. A cackle that froze her blood. The steps above stopped as Moss and Damien cursed at the witch's untimely arrival.

"Keep her busy at all costs," Moss commanded Damien.

"I'll do my best—just get Beth to safety," Damien beseeched, sounding nearly as concerned as Moss.

Beth still had to make amends to Damien. He hurt, and she didn't want him to take sole responsibility for what had happened between them. It was what it was, no more, no less. He lived a reclusive life, and she sensed the deep loneliness that surrounded him.

The high-pitched laugh went silent far too quickly for things to be good. Beth's gut screamed to prepare for some bad shit coming at her. Sure enough, the small ledge she perched on gave way beneath her.

Chapter Seventeen

The horrid sensation of free falling set in again, but the scream hadn't even passed her trembling lips before a steely arm clamped about her waist, thankfully tight. So damn tight, in fact, she feared air wouldn't be able to enter her lungs again.

Moss had her. She loved the feeling of being safe in his secure embrace.

Then they slammed against the unyielding stone of the cave's interior wall with such force an audible *swoosh,* followed by a whack, ricocheted around them.

"Are you unharmed?" Moss asked when they'd finally stilled.

"Uh, yeah. Yes," she managed to eke out between pained gasps. "Don't suppose you've ever watched *George of the Jungle?*"

"Who?"

"Never mind. I'm a bit delirious, I think."

"Climb onto my back and wrap your legs about my waist. Can you do this, Beth?"

She glanced down, which turned out to be a huge mistake. Huge.

She couldn't see a thing, only pitch blackness, and realized only one thing kept her from plunging into the darkness. An arm. One large, muscular arm that happened to be attached to an equally muscular body belonging to Moss. Though she trusted Moss, the thought was still quite disconcerting. She didn't doubt Moss's capabilities, but she'd rather not test her theories about his strength and endurance.

She carefully shifted her arms to reach up around his neck, and even in the dark, she could make out the subtle glow of his special, nocturnal eyes. Their glinting apparently allowed him keen vision even through the darkest of darks. Though she lacked his visual gift, she knew the moment they'd locked eyes. Felt it in her soul. His beckoning for her to do what needed to be done and trust in him.

"You must move quickly as I fear Octavia's quick return," he whispered, urging her onto him by nudging her thigh with his.

Using his shoulders as anchors, she hoisted herself higher, climbing his body like a ladder. Once they were pelvis to pelvis, she wrapped her legs around his waist and locked her ankles. Once Beth was secure, Moss began the climb back up. She could do no more than hold tight, rest her head upon his sculpted back, and pray like hell.

Once they'd reached the top and were back to where she could see a damn thing, she noted the extreme worry marring his beautiful face. Moss had been that frightened for her? Or was it perhaps fear of the witch's wrath? She hoped for the first, but after his dismay at what he deemed her betrayal, she wasn't positive, only hoping.

She didn't have long to wait for her answer. He pulled her roughly against him, and his lips came down on hers. She no longer had any doubts. This was a claiming. A marking of one's territory, of possession, and she readily embraced him.

Her heart soared. Moss still wanted her. So much so, he'd marked her, and witch or no witch, her world suddenly felt right. As if a part of her had always been missing until she'd found him.

Moss completed her. With him she became whole.

Her tongue swept past his, their breathing ragged and needy while the evidence of his increased desire pressed hard against her belly. What she wouldn't give for another magical night with Moss at his secluded, rustic cabin.

Okay, shack. Whatever. If Moss lived in it, as far as she was concerned it was the Taj freaking Mahal.

One arm encircled her waist while the other pressed up under her ass, forcing her to wrap her legs about his waist once again.

This time, under entirely better circumstances. Their lips were still locked when she felt the sharp chill on her back where he used the cave's wall to assist help him control their position.

She edged her hands under his shirt, seeking out the cool touch of his skin. Where most men would feel warm, Moss's reptilian side kept his body temperature a bit cooler than the norm, and she could care less. In fact, she found it rather exotic. The sensation of his cool skin as it slid against hers brought tingles over the surface of her skin.

He continued his urgent thrusts, and she was about to say the hell with it and strip his pants off right then and right there. The witch could kiss her royal ass. He was Beth's, and only Beth's. Ms. Skankass needed to find her own boyfriend. Maybe a skunk.

But getting jiggidity against the cave wall probably wouldn't be the best idea right then. As if Moss had come to the same sad conclusion, he reluctantly released her legs but continued pinning her with his body. Head bowed, he struggled to regain control, thus allowing her to try to control the shaking in her legs. She understood his reluctance to let her go. If they stayed together, no one had the power to tear them apart. Beth didn't want to let go any more than he did, but they needed to boogie somewhere safe.

"That was highly wrong of me," he whispered as his lips brushed her ear. "To endanger you again in such a way. We need to get moving. I need to get you to safety. Get you back home."

He sounded firm, yet sadness resonated at the mere thought of them parting once again. Sheer determination forced her to step away so she would be able to get eye to eye with him when she explained they would not be parting again anytime soon. Octavia was a powerful witch capable of getting to Beth no matter where she hid. It would be better if they stuck together. Plus after the last time they'd parted, bad shit came down. On all of them.

"Moss, I'm not leaving you, but you're right about the home part. However, you, my friend are coming with me."

"I cannot," he stated gruffly before looking elsewhere about the cave. His gaze held longing and hope locked deep within.

"And why can't you? My home not good enough for you?" She hoped to lure him with the pretense he'd offended her. She even propped a hand on her jutting hip as she impatiently waited for his reply.

"No, I meant no disrespect to your home. I am sure it is a lovely, warm place. I…I no longer fit in your world. Now we must go," he stated purposefully, trying to close the subject from further discussion.

Dude, don't piss me off.

Moss tried to pull her with him, but she dug her heels into the hard dirt floor and refused to budge.

"You can fit in, Moss. I'm not saying you have to jump right back into society, but you have as much right to join it as any of the rest of us."

"You are wrong, my sweet, innocent Beth." The forlorn look he gave her broke her heart, for it reflected absolute resolve. He was resigned to staying in the swamps and accepting his punishment for something he didn't do. It hurt her heart and pissed her off all at once.

"No, I am not wrong." She stomped a foot for emphasis. "Moss, what makes you so sure you don't belong?"

He shoved away from her before jerking off his shirt, ripping it to shreds in the process. He motioned to his tattoo-style scales.

"These. Are you to tell me the rest of society has changed so much, they too now bear scales over their bodies? Am I that mistaken in what the world has become?" he challenged.

"No, maybe they don't. But those don't mean you can't fit in. Hell, Moss, it doesn't mean you even need to try to fit in. Damn it, you can at least rejoin the living," she exclaimed, exasperated at trying to get him to see the light. Desperate to show him the error in his thinking. To ensure she wouldn't lose him after everything they'd gone through.

"I am alive," he all but whispered.

"No, Moss. No, you're not. You haven't been living in a long time and you know it. You've hidden out here in the swamps and existed, not lived. Please come with me. Please let me help you," she begged.

"Uh, guys…hate to interrupt this tender moment and all, but we've got company," Damien shouted down the tunnel to them.

Hell. She'd all but forgotten about Damien's presence.

"How convenient and thoughtful of you," Octavia screeched. "The gang's all here in one nice, tidy package. Ready to die, Beth?"

"Well, someone had their Cheerios pissed in," Beth tarted, ready to square off with the witch once and for all.

Moss took up a protective stance in front of her. Guarding her, protecting her, and even though the situation was bleak, Beth beamed from ear to ear, proud her swamp warrior stood next to her. Well, in front for now, but Beth knew soon they'd battle side-by-side.

Part of her wanted to stick out her tongue at Octavia while chanting, "Nanny nanny boo boo," right before giving Moss's firm ass a squeeze. Rub in what she had access to and the old bitch didn't, and never would again. Thankfully, her better self gained control.

She caught Damien sneaking up behind Octavia while the witch's attention was on them. Beth wasn't sure what Damien had in mind, but before Damien managed whatever he'd planned, a loud, angry shriek pierced the cave as Octavia whirled in the narrow passageway to face him.

Octavia raised a threatening hand. A shimmery blue light radiated from her fingertips as a storm erupted around them. One would swear a tornado had arrived, with the chaos generated. Sudden, gale-force winds came whipping down the tunnel, picking up loose sand from the cave's floor. The debris stung as particles embedded in Beth's skin. Moss, too, whirled, and before the stings from the sand could do any real damage, his body sheltered hers. Moss's scales formed a protective barrier around him she prayed would protect him from whatever was happening.

She embraced Moss, thankful for his protection, but she feared for Damien's well being too. If what they felt was merely the after effects of what Octavia was doling out to Damien, he couldn't be faring too well.

She tried to shield her eyes enough to peek around Moss's massive frame, but with all the flying dust bunnies from hell, her attempt proved useless. She hoped Damien would be all right.

Another ear-piercing shriek sprang forth, so high-pitched Beth actually thought her eardrums would burst. This shriek seemed to radiate even more rage than the last, and the surrounding stone enhanced the god-awful sound.

She again tried to see what played out behind them, but now it wasn't the sand that was the issue, but a weird, blinding white light so intense she had no choice but to close her eyes and turn her head. When the light retreated, both she and Moss instinctively put their guards up for whatever drama the witch had pulled now.

Beth's jaw hit the ground. For there in the center, where the bright light had just been, stood her aunt. And to say Grace looked pissed was a huge understatement. *Huge.*

"Aunt Grace?" Beth asked in shock, fearful this was yet another of the witch's tricks.

"Well, sweetness, who else would it be?" Grace cocked her hip out with attitude and braced her hand on it. A most definite Grace move.

"Uh, well, I don't know, but how, why?" Beth stuttered.

"We can get around to all the particulars later, dear. For now let's concentrate on taking care of the old bitch once and for all, shall we?" Grace's strong essence was awe-inspiring. She wasn't rattled in the slightest.

The light Grace had emerged from still swirled slightly as

did the debris from the dirt floor. But Beth could make out that Octavia had vanished.

"Your mother raised you better than that," Grace tsked.

"Excuse me?" Beth asked, more bewildered by the second at her aunt's sudden but welcome appearance.

"Aren't you going to introduce me to your handsome young friend?"

If it were possible, Beth's jaw would have dropped open even farther. She began to wonder if, somewhere along the way, she'd landed in Oz. The lollipop kids would be next to show, as they welcomed her to Munchkin Land and offered her a giant candy while gathering around her to sing and dance.

Hell, why not? They already had the Wicked Witch of the West. Maybe Aunt Grace was really Glenda the good Witch of the East. Oh, God...she really had lost her mind.

"Uh, okay. Moss, meet my Aunt Grace. Aunt Grace this is my, err...friend, Moss." She almost bit her tongue off to keep from saying "boyfriend" but as it was, Aunt Grace cast a wary glance toward him. Moss, thankfully, seemed not to have noticed her uncertainty on how to announce him and stood in his usual, self-assured manner.

"No, dearest, your other handsome friend." Aunt Grace flung her hand in the opposite direction and, pivoting on her heel, locked eyes with the battle-weary Damien.

"Damien?" Beth shot a wayward glance toward Damien, who still brushed away debris from his entanglement with the old hag. Realizing the conversation had turned to him, he paused and took interest in why. He stood just off from the abyss she nearly fell into, with Grace between him, Moss and her. The corridor was narrow, but wound through the cave to God only knew where.

"I, oh...he's..."

"A friend of mine," Moss answered.

Beth was relieved to hear Moss claim Damien as friend once again. She wasn't sure if they had been friends prior, but she sensed they hadn't been enemies. She wouldn't have relished any more physical fallout between the two on her account.

"Let me introduce myself. I am Damien, and you, no doubt, are the exquisite Aunt Grace." Damien bowed slightly before taking Aunt Grace's hand in his and sweeping a light kiss across her knuckles.

Beth smiled, watching Damien, who actually appeared to be flirting. After everything that had just gone down, he was openly flirting with her aunt. Most curious yet was the way Aunt Grace it was responding. Her sweet, innocent aunt stunned her by acting all swoony. Beth watched the interaction between the two and knew her beloved aunt needed some male attention. Hell, maybe she had for quite some time.

Chapter Eighteen

They only had a few moments before all hell broke loose again. Though they couldn't see her, it was obvious Octavia had returned by the smothering presence of evil permeating the dank cave. No doubt madder than all get out.

"Where the hell did you send her?" Beth whispered to Grace.

"I didn't send her anywhere. Apparently the collision of our magic's threw her off guard. She must have left until she knew what was happening." Grace offered.

Beth's hair stood on end. The others had sensed the witch's return as well, by the wary stances they took. All went stock still as they scanned the dark recesses of the tunnel ahead of them. Only a few candles still flickered behind them in the tunnel, making visibility difficult at best. Octavia might have been out of sight, but they knew she was ready to strike.

"I want all three of you out of here this instant," Grace whispered with an edge to her voice that left little room to argue.

"No way I'm leaving you," Beth answered, standing her ground.

"Nor am I," Damien declared, leaving only Moss.

"I do not wish for you to remain." Moss growled in full agreement with Grace.

"Ahh, I like this one." Grace grinned from ear to ear that Moss had agreed with her.

Pfft.

"Good thing you do, because right now I'm not real sure I do." Livid didn't come close to how Beth felt. This was her aunt, her blood. And her hero chose now to go all cavemanish? What happened to the man who dove head first into a bottomless pit to save her? The same man who used his own body to shield her?

So her he-man doubted her ability to take care of herself, did he? Well, she'd show him. Boy, would she ever.

"I do not mean to hurt your feelings, but your aunt is right—this is no place for you." Moss hated his next words; they made his stomach turn, but he would not let Beth down again. "Damien, take Beth to safety. I will stay with Grace and battle Octavia."

"All right, buddy, we need to set a few ground rules. First, you do not speak for me. I have my own voice, thank you very much. Second, drop the caveman shit. You're quite frankly pissing the shit out of me." Beth shook, as angry as hell.

"Uh, guys, hate to be a killjoy," Damien broke in, "but I don't think this is the time to be arguing. Something stanky this way comes." Damien backed up, sensing Octavia's presence coming closer.

"Beth, if you insist on ignoring my warnings, at least have the good sense to get behind Moss. Please," Grace begged, moving forward to stand closer to Damien.

Both her aunt and Damien stood in battle mode, and Beth had never seen her aunt like this before. Powerful, demanding, and all business. Wow, her aunt had been holding a lot back through the years. They'd have to have a little chat later, including how her aunt had found her.

As per her aunt's instructions, Moss positioned himself right in front of Beth. He was protective, overbearing, and pig-headed, and she loved her swamp man. But she wasn't an invalid and was damned tired of everyone treating her as such. She had powers too. Okay, not really powers more like little burps with bite… sometimes.

Freaky, hiss-like sounds slithered closer, as did the unusual sound of…barking? What in the hell? Making matters worse, the sound came from in front of and behind them. The minimal lighting from the few candles that had remained lit went out, plunging them into darkness.

"Damien, can you make them out?" Moss whispered.

"Got 'em in my sights. Geez, that's a whole lot of leather."

"Who? What? Leather? Damn it, you guys, what's coming?" Beth feared their answer.

"Sweetie, I don't think you want to know."

"What? You see them too?" she asked her aunt, surprised yet again.

"No, but I skimmed Damien's mind. Let's just say your appreciation of reptiles will come in handy," her aunt whispered.

Whoa, Nelly. There were massive differences between her bog man and true reptiles like snakes or…

Beth screamed when something cool and slimy brushed against her bare leg. Before she could stop herself, she'd climbed up Moss's back like some squeamish girl. Yeah, perfect way to prove she was as badass as they were. Lovely. She'd never live this down, she thought, arms around his neck, legs around his waist, clinging on for dear life as Moss whirled them around with no warning.

"How many do you detect?" Moss questioned Damien.

"Far too many. You?"

"Same."

Oh, this sucked. If two swamp shifters seemed unnerved at what headed their way, shit had to be bad. Though the timing was bad to be wondering about such things, she couldn't help but remember Moss's quip to Damien about road kill. What the hell kind of shifter was Damien?

"Armor up, old friend," Moss stated, though Beth didn't understand what he meant.

"Already done."

"Moss, can I ask you a question?" Beth whispered, no longer caring if the timing sucked.

"Do you see something?"

"Err, no, but I'm curious."

"Do not worry, Beth. I will get you and your aunt out of here unscathed."

"Well, though that's an ideal plan, that's not my question," she clarified, still scanning the darkness to try to see what they all did.

"What is your question?"

From draped across his back, she leaned closer, placing her mouth by his ear. "What kind of shifter is Damien?" Moss stilled for a moment.

"That isn't my secret to tell. I am sorry. I do not wish to withhold from you, but it would be wrong to tell, if he has not."

Though dying from curiosity, she understood Moss's reluctance to divulge Damien's secret. Truthfully, now was not the time to be asking trivial shit, as evidenced by the commotion coming from Grace and Damien's last location.

"Hope I haven't kept you waiting long," Octavia cackled, hovering in the air above the pit Moss had rescued Beth from. Octavia's black gown floated about her like a nasty oil slick, moving about as if carried by its own will.

"Nah, had enough time to finish my nails," Grace spat. Damn, but Beth liked this sassy new side of her Grace.

"I must say I'm quite disappointed in you, Damien. But I will forgive this latest indiscretion if you simply ask nicely. I even promise no retribution of any kind. In fact, I'm a little turned on by this new, dominant side you've hidden. Might make for an interesting playtime."

Damien gagged, Beth assumed over memories of being with the bitch.

Beth caught something flittering through her mind. Voices. She closed her eyes and concentrated. *But if he could get close enough, stall her long enough, maybe the others would have time to leave.* She'd picked up Damien's thoughts. Wow, this had never happened before. Then more tickling started—Grace's voice warning Damien that Octavia would use him to immobilize the rest.

As sudden as things had gone dark, the candles flickered once again to life, though she almost wished they hadn't. The floor moved with life. Snakes slithered everywhere, and if she wasn't mistaken…

"Grace, look out!" Beth screamed in warning as an eight-foot alligator began skulking her way.

"Oh, don't mind Sebastian—he's all bark and little bite. A rare mistake." Octavia seemed to get lost in thought for a moment, looking down at the eight-foot, scaled monster, which seemed a bit lost itself. Himself? Instinct told her the creature would rip anyone to shreds, including Octavia if given half a chance. Her aunt stood frozen in place, caught between the gator and Damien. Damien stood between the gator and Octavia, leaving Beth and Moss behind them all. Which, to Beth, meant in a much better position to attack as they were the least visible.

Octavia returned her attentions to them. Her gaze narrowed when it passed over Damien, and tightened even further when it stopped on Moss. Clearly, she was pissed he hadn't darted to her side like a good little reptile shifter.

"You will live to regret your decision and betrayal." Though she hadn't indicated whom she addressed, Moss hissed.

Out of the corner of her eye, Beth caught her aunt swinging her hand in a shooing motion. Grace wanted them to move back, away from the gator and Octavia.

She glanced behind them then down. Wow, that was a mistake. The sight of a wiggling floor brought the shudders out. No, she didn't hate snakes, but that sure as hell didn't mean she wanted to be swimming through them, either. Blech.

"Son of a bitch!" Damien hissed, and she squinted to see that he kicked something before hopping around on one foot. "Damn thing bit me."

"A snake?" Grace gasped.

"No one of those damn little gators." Damien still hopped, but all could tell he was fine.

"You think he meant son of bitch literally?" Beth whispered in

Moss's ear, earning a quiet chuckle from her quiet giant.

"They may be small, but their bite packs a punch." Damien warned as each used their feet to shuffle the small reptiles away.

Shoving the creepy thoughts of the numerous things scurrying about below, Beth focused on figuring out what her aunt had up her sleeve. If Grace had a plan, they all needed to be in on it. Grace said she'd skimmed Damien's mind earlier, apparently seeing the snakes covering the floor. If Grace could skim Damien's mind, and Beth herself had caught tidbits from both, then maybe she'd be able to broadcast a message to her aunt. It was worth a shot at least.

Squeezing her hands in concentration, making fists that actually had her nails breaking her palms' surface, she telepathically tossed out her question.

What's the plan, Grace?

Damn, but this telepathy shit was hard with Octavia's scathing remarks and threats flying about in the background. The witch had one of those voices like nails on a chalkboard. Beth did her best to tune out everything, Continuing to broadcast her questions while envisioning Grace's face.

Finally, after what seemed an eternity, her aunt's clear voice came through. In no uncertain terms, Grace told her she and Moss needed to slowly back up. She planned to cause a partial cave-in. Grace hoped to knock the bitch down into the pit as the falling rocks effectively walled off the area.

Beth didn't understand how Grace intended to pull off the cave-in, but at least one of them had a solid plan. Slowly, she reached out and grasped Moss's hand and gave it a firm squeeze. Moss squeezed back, confirming he got the message something was up.

She slid off his back and gently tugged his arm, alerting him he needed to follow her. As he stepped back, so did she, matching his steps so neither appeared to have moved. Doing so was made difficult by the snakes and small gators littering the floor. Thank goodness, short of the eight-footer up by Grace, the rest of the gators seemed small enough they had to be babies. On one hand, good, on the other, Beth feared they were truly wild gators and not baby gator shifters. By all accounts, only handsome, grown men ended up on Octavia's menu. Wild meant they would have to tread carefully, as these gators lacked the human instincts locked inside, but were rather nature's creatures with their own set of survival and feeding rules.

Grace must have sent a mental message to Damien, as both she and Moss noted his sly moves in their direction. Grace obviously meant to unsettle Octavia with her remarks and Beth bet, hoped to catch her off guard.

"Oh, yeah, whoop dee do. You wham-bammed a few poor souls, trapping them here in your bug-infested home to do your sexual bidding and you think you're all that? What's the matter, Octavia So butt ugly you couldn't snag a man the old-fashioned way? Is that it? *Ohh*, it is?"

"Shut the fuck up. You know nothing about me, but I know everything about you."

"Oh, you do, do you?" Grace taunted, edging a bit closer to her.

"Cocky, aren't you? Well, let's test just how cocky you are. Does the name Henry Gerard ring a bell? Oh, my, I guess from that look, that's a yes?"

Though they continuing their slow movements backwards, Beth could tell Octavia had hit a nerve with Grace. Her aunt's back went ramrod straight, but so far, Grace hadn't made a peep in response to Octavia's last comment. Who was this Henry Gerard Octavia spoke of? Obviously, he hadn't just been someone her aunt was acquainted with. No, by her aunt's tense posture and changing aura, he'd been important to Grace. She'd cared for him deeply.

"They do say a picture is worth a thousand words. Let's test the theory, shall we?" Octavia's hands flew up in front of her, and she swirled them round and round until a glowing, golden-red haze enveloped Grace, who seemed unable to move or speak.

Beth watched in horror as Grace began trembling. She couldn't tell if her aunt's reaction stemmed from fear, rage, or a combination of both. Beth halted, and Moss too, as she tried in vain to grasp the severity of the situation. What had happened to the plan? Was Grace okay or had she, too, fallen under a spell of the witch?

Just as Beth went to reverse her course and head back toward Grace, she heard her aunt's sharp, rage-filled message ordering her to continue as she had been. Her tone was fierce, crisp, on edge, and worried Beth as to exactly who was unnerving whom.

Images of a handsome man projected from within the red haze and Grace gasped, falling to her knees.

"How sad. But on the bright side, I proved how quickly your one true love could be seduced. Don't worry about thanking me. I assure you, Henry was all my pleasure. Hours and hours' worth."

In the midst of the golden hue encircling Grace a brighter, bluish glow began. This glow didn't come from the witch, however. It came from Grace and grew brighter by the moment.

"Justice met is Justice served to those who've passed beyond their bode. I call you now to aid with those who've fought the same and refused to lose. Hear our cries and empower us to ensure free will against all those lost."

Beth, alongside Moss and Damien, stilled as the power of her aunt's words unleashed the now blinding, bluish glow. The light flooded the cavern, spilling forth into every tunnel, crack, and crevice. The power was undeniable and already causing instability as loose rocks began scattering down. By the time Octavia realized what Grace intended, it was too late. The power had built into such a force it had nowhere to retreat except within the rocks themselves.

Soon, boulder-sized chunks tumbled down, blocking Beth's view of Octavia and Grace.

With the wall erected, her aunt had succeeded. But at what price? Beth screamed Grace's name and broke from Moss's embrace, frantic to get to her beloved aunt.

Chapter Nineteen

Beth nearly throttled her aunt for scaring her like she had. Beth thought for sure she'd lost Grace in the cave-in, but she'd learned Grace had thrown a protection spell about them all before casting the power out toward Octavia. When the debris settled, there her aunt had stood without so much as a scratch on her. Where Octavia had gone, none knew, but regardless, it had bought them the time needed to escape the tunnels and get back to Grace's to plot their next course of action.

Once she'd returned from her shower, they sat around Grace's table with Moss looking more than a little apprehensive about his new surroundings. He'd never seen a microwave, an iPod, or the many other modern items, much less had an opportunity to toy with them.

His favorite? Well, of course, the television. To be fair, the giant, flat-screen plasma had also captured Damien's attention. What was it with men and giant televisions? Here were two men, unused to any real technology to speak of, and both were drawn like moths to a flame to the plasma.

Beth and Grace both sat back, rolling their eyes at how the boob tube could turn even the most rugged, outdoorsy men into drooling zombies. Beth had never guessed what a sense of humor Grace had until her aunt snatched the remote and jacked up the sound to max level right as both men went to tentatively touch it.

Priceless. Beth thought Grace would have to replace the roof, as high as each he-man jumped. She couldn't remember ever seeing Grace laugh so long or hard. Of course, after Damien put his fist through the plasma, she didn't laugh so much. But Beth still sensed the humor hiding behind the shock. Grace knew all too well life was far too short to sweat the small, replaceable stuff. Once they'd both managed to miraculously settle the two beasts down with a few grunts at having their newfound toys taken away, those being the remotes to several appliances in the home, Moss and Damien grew serious. Both spoke of their inside information regarding Octavia. Damien had discovered many others like themselves lost to the swamp's nocturnal magic. Lost to her dark magic. They explained what some of her weaknesses were, though neither had enough information to ensure ending the old battle-axe.

For the most part, Octavia had left Moss and Damien in the dark, but they'd caught whispers in the swamp of one who had escaped her clutches. The one that chose an eternal life as a swamp creature over being a cross between the two, neither wholly man nor beast.

And to that one poor soul, the secrets of the witch and swamp had been released. Her magic stemmed from the essence of the swamp itself. The place she'd been born into, the place she called home, and the place where, when her time came, she would meet her maker.

Grace's eyes moistened at the mention of this other creature. A wistful, faraway sadness quickly darkened the shine in them. Beth wasn't the only one to see it. Both men and, as if in unity, the three sat in a moment of silence. A moment to honor those who'd fallen to the fates of dark magic and mortal hatreds.

"You knew this other? The one who gave up his fight and chose to remain one with the swamp?" Damien spoke in a soft, soothing tone as his eyes sought her aunt's.

The two stared quietly at one another, as if reading the other's thoughts. Grace's subtle sadness took on much darker hues as their silence stretched. Beth glanced at Moss. A small nod of his head acknowledged he was aware of the private moment transpiring between the two.

"Yes, I know of the rumored one and his choice all too well. We were to have been married before he was stolen from me."

Her voice had been little above a whisper, but the fiery rage born from pain burned in the depths of Grace's eyes was intense. Beth understood then what Grace had left out. Her love had ultimately chosen the swamp over her.

There was so much about her aunt that she'd ever dreamed. So many deeply faceted layers under what had appeared on the outside to be a normal woman. And now Beth's heart broke for her, as had Grace's all those years ago.

Though Grace wore a perfect poker face, clear and evident pain still radiated from her. She had loved and bitterly lost, and the scars would forever remain. Invisible, but there, just under the surface.

Beth noticed Damien's demeanor had gone icy as he studied Grace with serious scrutiny. Worry appeared to adorn his tanned, weathered features. A look of camaraderie passed between them. Damien had lost someone too, which explained the loneliness she'd picked up from him back at his chamber.

She was relieved when Moss's strong hand encased hers. The grip settled her. Put her heart a little at ease, though he had the same faraway look the others bore. It didn't take a rocket scientist to know he was remembering his own losses.

Here she sat, with three people all deeply affected by the cold, calculating brutality of one mean-ass witch. The more she observed their pained silence, the angrier she grew. The angrier she grew, the more determined she became to make the bitch pay in some equally painful and lengthy way.

"What was his name?" Beth hoped talking about him would somehow bring Grace closure. She'd kept him a secret for too long. He might also be their secret weapon for destroying Octavia and bringing ultimate closure for them all.

"His name was Henry, and he was a brilliant herpetologist," Grace answered, holding her head high with pride and memory.

Beth smiled gently. She knew Grace would have to be pushed a bit to get the entire story from her. Beth hated having to do it, knowing how much pain the subject might cause, but she knew no way around it. She caught her aunt's understanding glance just before Grace took it upon herself to go into the details surrounding Henry's disappearance.

"I was nineteen to his thirty, but I didn't care about the age difference. His compassion and love for nature and all things innocent won my heart. We were engaged to be married. I planned our wedding while he worked on his thesis. He'd made plans to camp out in the swamp over the weekend. I was actually to have joined him, but at the last moment, I canceled."

Her voice cracked when she spoke the word *canceled*. Beth reached out with the intention of holding her aunt's hand, but was beaten in doing so by none other than Damien. Instead, she patted her aunt's shoulder. Odd as it was, she felt a strange surge of energy and relief pour through Grace at the first contact with Damien.

After taking a moment to collect herself, Grace cleared her throat and continued, all the while clutching Damien's hand in support. Damien's thumb never stopped stroking the top of Grace's hand.

"He was to have returned late Sunday evening, so when he didn't call me that evening, I thought nothing of it. I just assumed he'd either arrived home very late or decided to stay through the evening and leave the next morning. When he still hadn't called by Monday evening, I became worried sick. I checked his classes and found he had not made it to any of them. I immediately started calling his friends, but he hadn't been in contact with any of them. By Tuesday, I convinced the local law enforcement to begin searching for him. After weeks of searches, they presumed he'd ventured to close to the water's edge, and one of the many swamp predators struck."

Her voice trailed off, growing so soft Beth could scarcely make out her words. Tears welled as Grace told of her heartbreak.

"I knew, though. Beyond a shadow of a doubt, I knew he was alive if nothing else. I *felt* that much. But I couldn't convince anyone else of this, and all searches were called off and he was declared dead. His death was ruled accidental."

Beth watched as Grace turned toward Moss and Damien, caught the hope written on her face that just maybe they'd heard how his life had been. Or maybe she thought they might know what had caused him to give up? What animal had he become and chosen to remain as? Could they communicate with it? Him? Had they already done so? Were they friends? At least those were the questions she thought she'd have, if she were Grace.

Both men locked eyes with one another as a silent agreement passed between them. Moss solemnly spoke.

"I never met your Henry, but he sounds like a fine gentleman. If, as was told to me, he became one with the swamps, I assure you of his happiness, for he has a place to belong. You cannot know the anguish of not belonging somewhere. Being stuck in between worlds, being able to call neither your own, is a hell in itself." Beth saw Moss's sorrow-filled eyes, while taking in her aunt's demeanor as his words sank in. Words meant to help ease Grace's pain, and Beth appreciated him all the more for them.

Damien chimed in next, but he did so privately. He stood while still clasping Grace's hand and urged Grace to follow him. Beth started to rise as well, but Moss shook his head subtly in a plea for her to remain behind.

She waited until Damien and Grace disappeared out onto the porch and into the setting sun before turning to ask Moss what was up. "What is it you two aren't saying?" She feared what he'd say.

"Some of us—of the swamp, that is—know *of* each other. Some of us, as in the case of Damien and I, have even met. But there are some who are more legend than real. Henry was one such legend. A legend I'm afraid didn't have a happy ending."

"But you said..." she began, feeling quite confused.

"I know what I said, but I saw her pain, and as I've no proof to the rumors, I didn't want to add to her heartache," he answered with a tone that implied his own painful memories were still in the forefront of his mind.

"Okay, go ahead and tell me then. What did you hear about Henry?"

"He did find the key to her spell, the key that allowed him to become one with the swamp. More specifically, becoming fully, the inner animal he'd carried inside. That much is true. However, she used her other swamp slaves to hunt him down, luring him into her trap. Her rage was like none had ever seen. He was never seen again. Neither the man nor the beast."

"Oh. shit. But there's no proof she killed him, right?"

"None, I'm afraid. I know your aunt needs closure, but I cannot give her any. That said, Damien knows others like us and can ask if anyone has heard anything as of late."

"There truly is a whole other world going on out there in the swamps, isn't there?" she murmured, awestruck at how clueless she'd been.

"Yes, there is, though it's a very sad and obscure world for the most part. The swamp holds beautiful and mystical qualities. Gifts from nature herself, but there is also the dark side. That is where Octavia rules."

He laid a calming hand on her knee, and it was then that she realized she'd been swinging her crossed leg in tune with her mind. Which, at the moment, happened to be racing with ideas on where to start in her plans for vengeance. Of course, her mind was also out on the porch wondering what was going on between Grace and Damien. Like whether her aunt was okay. Whether Damien offered her comfort and exactly how much comfort he offered.

Then Moss gently squeezed her knee, grabbing her attention. Though they'd just nearly died, and for the most part had broken up, her libido spiked when she saw the spark in his eyes and the flare of his nose as he seemed to be…smelling her?

"Moss, I really think I need to explain…about earlier, with Damien."

"Damien already did. I acted like—what did you say? A pompous ass?"

"Yeah, uh, that I did." She didn't add all the other names she'd considered.

"The thought of his hands…his eyes on you, I can't explain. I just lost it."

"I really, truly thought I was with you." Gah, she didn't want to go into details at just what she'd done, thinking she was with him.

"I was hard-headed. I did know what Octavia was capable of. Damien acted rightly. I wouldn't have wanted you in pain or medical danger. The man chose well, and I owe him."

They'd been through so much, and the timing was shitty, but she needed him, and now. Glancing out to the porch, she could tell Grace and Damien were deep in conversation, so she turned to Moss once more. She saw the fire and hunger raging within and gently pulled him to standing. That was all the encouragement he needed.

"I need you, Beth. I need to be with you, in you." There was no mistaking the urgency in his voice. It shook with need, and warmth flooded her center. She needed him too, she admitted as she led him to the guest room.

So much had been revealed this night, and Beth knew deep down by the time it was over, none of them would ever be the same again.

Chapter Twenty

Grace leaned against the wooden rail of her back deck, wrapping her arms about her waist, soaking in the serenity of the moonlight cascading over the still swamp waters. Her emotions were still unstable from the fresh pain of ripping open old wounds.

Where would life have taken her if things had been different? Would she have had children? Girls or boys? Maybe she would have been lucky enough to have one of each. Whimsical thoughts of what life might have been like began to engulf her. Visions of a dream family gathered on the deck enjoying all the mysterious beauty of the swamp.

Life was a bitch, and the bitch had landed a full-out whammy on her. But what happened, happened. She thought she'd run out of tears years ago. How wrong she'd been.

Damien sensed her turmoil and pain as Grace, deep in thought, stared out into the swamp. Quiet, he approached and brought his hands to her shoulders, giving them a tentative squeeze on the knots forming in her muscles. When she made no objection, he began kneading the stress from them. Her small sigh of pleasure was all the thanks he needed.

Grace's head lolled from side to side as Damien worked pure magic into her aching body. The stress melted away, leaving her boneless. Something about this man spoke to her on a level she hadn't experienced since Henry. Different, almost mythical. If only they'd met at another time in her life, preferably when she'd been younger and not as cynical.

*

They'd made love and reconnected. They'd both needed it. That something which she could only assume, placed his scent on her once more. In comments from Damien, she'd known he'd detected some imprint from Moss but hadn't felt he'd had a choice but to ignore the others warning. Even still, and beyond the sexual need, Beth understood Moss's desire to lay claim. Relished in the fact he'd still wanted to after everything that had happened.

Being with Moss again was every bit as euphoric as it had been before. His cock embedded deeply within her, his large body caging hers within his, and that freaking amazing tongue of his. Wow. He nuzzled into her neck, and she suspected he wanted to bite her again but then his teeth merely grazed the area, rather than actually bite. Either way, that little nip where the shoulder and neck meet, lit every nerve on fire as everything within her exploded. Her thighs had gripped his hips as the purposeful pace he'd kept spiraled into an all-out frenzy of mating. Once spent, they'd lain in each other's arms and simply taken solace in the moment. Neither knew what the future would hold, but for now, they were together.

Beth knew it was only a matter of time before Grace and Damien would come knocking soon, but they'd needed the bonding.

Moss rose, a bit distant, and dressed in silence. One moment rage filled his face, and in the next, sorrow rose, tinted with traces of happiness. Bittersweet. His breathing grew ragged, as if on the verge of panic. Too many emotions too fast she realized as he paced the room looking very much the tiger in a very small cage.

"Penny for your thoughts," Beth said. He worried her.

"All these years of believing I had committed a wrong against the poor children and my wife. Now to learn their lives went on. Do you..."

Even though he'd trailed off, she knew what he'd been about to ask. Did she have information about what had happened to his wife? Yes. She knew a little, but she wouldn't be able to tell him if his wife had experienced any joys. It would be a complicated answer at best. He wouldn't relish the fact she'd survived their nightmare in the swamp only to pass away a few years later from probable heartache.

"I need some air. I'll be back in a while." His voice was gruff and left no room for debate. Not that she would, as he needed his alone time to process his past. She did too, as she tried to push away the hurt of his aching for another. No matter how she wished to help him, this was a ghost he had to make peace with for himself.

She gave him a silent nod, realizing she'd become the last man standing, so to speak. Heading out to the deck to check on Grace and Damien, she made a quick U-turn when, at the storm door, she noticed the intimacy between the two. She found no need to interrupt the duo. If her aunt needed Damien's massage and some male sympathy, more power to her.

With everyone preoccupied, the cabin fell deathly silent. She decided a little research was in order and veered toward the hidden library housing the special books. The location was a secret and only shared by immediate and competent family members.

The closet door in Grace's room opened on silent hinges, and Beth gave a hard whack to the interior wall. There was a faint, familiar creak as the secret passageway opened up before her. Moving by memory, Beth wound her way through the dark to her favorite place as a child.

The small, circular room housed the books of their craft, a small reading table, and one comfy sitting chair. On the table sat an antique oil lamp and a small box of matches. Nothing whatsoever had changed in this room, as if time had no meaning or place here.

She lit the lamp and began searching for one particular book. The book of mirrored magic. Mirrored magic contained unbinding spells. In layman's terms, the book contained spells to counteract dark magic.

Finding the well-worn, ancient book, she blew the dust off its cracked bindings and curled up in the plush chair. It wasn't long before she began drifting. It had been a long few days with very little sleep, and though she hadn't planned to, she nodded off.

She awoke with a start and a sense someone had awakened her on purpose. She could have sworn she'd been shaken. Stretching, she sat up and took note of the mirror book's marked page. Odd—she didn't remember leaving the book open. Stranger still was the spell on the opened, dog-eared page. The spell of redundancy—a strong spell with multiple methods and purposes. There were also a few eraser spells handwritten among them, however, those appeared to be in a different language. Beth hoped Grace would be able to elaborate further on the contents and sort out the helpful ones. A shiver sped through her, as if someone spied on her. Beth couldn't shake the sense that more than chance played a role in her waking to find the book open to those two pages.

She'd exited Grace's closet, spellbook in tow, when a vision hit. Though clouded and vague, it left her with a gut-wrenching sickness. Beth had been able to make out Octavia, Grace, and Damien. All three were back in Damien's cave and two were battling, fiercely so. Sprawled across Damien's bed, the lifeless body of Moss lay face down in bloodied sheets. Taking in the paleness of his body, Beth feared him dead.

Her sporadic visions didn't always come true, and never provided a time frame. What she'd seen could have been a year from now, or even tomorrow. Beth had no idea, and that was the worst thing about her visions—the uncertainty of when.

Shaken by the gore she'd witnessed, she didn't realize Moss had been standing in the doorway, or that he'd come to stand in front of her, until she shook off the vision and saw him.

Startled, she screamed and dropped the book. "Oh, my God," She choked.

"What?" he urged. "You've gone pale." He grabbed for her hand. "And clammy."

She looked him in the eyes, thought about lying about what she'd witnessed, and knew to do so would be pointless. As dangerous a threat as Octavia had become, not telling him about the graphic imagery she'd seen, wasn't an option.

"I think I saw your death." Speaking the words brought tears to her eyes and crushed her heart as bad as if someone reached into her chest and gripped it within a mighty fist.

"And this brings you such sorrow merely saying it?" he whispered.

"Damn it, Moss…what do you think?" she spat, angry he'd ever question such crap. Her flesh rose as goose bumps spread over her, and she began to shake uncontrollably.

He drew her into his arms. "Ssshh, do not cry. We will defeat Octavia together. I shall not allow further harm to come to you. I want nothing more than to protect and cherish you."

"It's not me I'm worried about. I don't want to lose you." She sniffed. Wow, so not a sexy sound. "But feel free to cherish me all you want."

She nuzzled into his chest, situating herself better in his embrace. Soon, her tremors subsided and a firm hand at the small of her back pressed her body into his. He'd needed no further signals to figure out what she wanted…again.

Oblivious to where they were, they fell into a perfectly timed rhythm with one another, each feeding off the other's movements like a well-choreographed tango. His lips claimed hers, and she accepted his claiming, longed for it as badly as he.

Beth felt the wall smack her in the ass, as he had somehow maneuvered them against it. Sex up against a wall would be a first and one she couldn't wait to try. She snickered wickedly at the decadent thought as the terror from earlier dissipated. Moss, paused at her little snicker, his own naughty thoughts reflected from his eyes, his previous intense demeanor gone. They were lost in the here and now with no haunted past taunting them.

His arms bracketed her body, and he leaned forward, keeping her immobile. His fingers went to her jaw and urged her head up until she opened her eyes.

She looked questioningly at him, mewling at the desperate need to connect with him again as she tossed a leg around his and gyrated her hips. The vision had shaken her badly, and she wanted to feel every inch of him. Prove he was here, alive and safe with her. Yet he refused to budge. He froze, pinning her effectively between the wall and himself, and simply stared into her eyes. Sought something within hers.

Then the corner of his mouth curved upwards, and the green in his eyes darkened, becoming predatory. His body never moved an inch from hers, yet he dropped his hands to her dress and began inching the fabric up. One hand curled around the cotton fabric, holding it at her waist, while the other fisted the string to her thong and, with a small yank, ripped it clear off.

Instinct had her climbing his thighs to wrap her legs around his.

"You. Are. Mine," he growled before he pulled back enough to enter her swiftly and in one hard stroke.

She let go of all the negativity. Let go of every inhibition she'd ever had. Clasped onto Moss and all the strength and security he offered. More than anything, the love he now revealed to her.

Nothing else in the world mattered at the moment except knowing what they shared went far more than just a one-night stand. And she was fairly certain he now believed her about his wife and the children's survival that night. Maybe within that truth he could release his past enough to embrace his future.

Their future?

Another deep thrust jolted her to serenity. His tongue engaged with hers, taunting it to come play. Her lips slipped back and forth across his as she nipped him playfully here and there, before sucking in his bottom lip and shivering when he moaned.

He shuddered around her as he fought to remain in control. She bit her own lip to keep from crying out. How quickly Moss could bring her to the edge still mystified her. Hell, when he shot her those hungry looks of his, she grew wet on the spot.

"Let go," he whispered when her inner walls began fluttering, the sure sign of her impending release.

His husky words proved too much. She bit the palm of her hand to prevent the scream that so wanted its freedom, remembering at the last moment they weren't alone. Damien and her aunt were somewhere in the cabin, or just outside.

Her legs clamped tightly about him, and her nails suddenly bit into his shoulders as she thrashed in the throes of ecstasy. Only then did she feel him let go and the beast rise.

While she'd fought for quiet, he had no issues with such. Grunts and growls erupted as he unleashed a mating fury.

He whispered how the beast recognized its mate. Through his panting, he managed something about needing to mark her…and then he bit into her shoulder. Hard enough her shoulder would reflect his mark, but shy of breaking the skin.

Granted, it shocked her a bit, but the possessive nature of the bite caused another orgasm to slam into her. She knew she was being claimed and loved it.

After all the years of feeling second rate, second best, she'd been chosen.

She—was—first.

Once they calmed their raging hormones, they did a quick clean-up and made their way toward the living room. She blushed at the very thought of having to face Grace and Damien. Hopefully they'd been outside and wouldn't be aware of what they'd been up to.

As they rounded the corner from the darkened hall into the quaint living quarters, Moss gave her hand an added squeeze. Just that little something she needed to calm her nerves and remind her of their secret tryst.

To her surprise, the living room was still deserted. How long had Damien and her aunt been out on the porch? A tingling zinged through her, warning her all was not right. Danger lurked near.

"Moss, something's off," she whispered.

"What do you mean, off?" Moss froze at her words of warning, throwing a protective arm in front of her.

"Something feels wrong, like when you have a déjà vu. You can remember something, but not necessarily what." She'd never quite been able to describe the buzz she got before her internal alarms went off.

Moss's posture went rigid, and Beth sensed he'd come to the same conclusion.

"She's been here." He had no need to explain who he meant.

Chapter Twenty-One

"Grace!" Screaming, Beth bolted past Moss's protection, desperation for her aunt's well being fueling her every move. She only managed a few steps before Moss efficiently tossed her over his shoulder for safekeeping.

"Let me go," she hissed, kicking and clawing every square inch of him she could reach.

"You will remain here. I will go check out back. Don't forget, Damien was with her. I saw how he looked at her. He won't allow any harm to come to her."

Beth didn't waste time arguing; deep down she knew he was right. She'd sensed the kinship between her aunt and Damien; actually she'd sensed a lot more than that, but what if Octavia or her minions had snuck up on them? What if Damien wasn't who he claimed to be? Octavia had whispered something to Damien back at the cave. Damien claimed not to have really wanted to kidnap Beth but had done so on Octavia's commands. Who was to say he wouldn't obey her orders again?

More than anything, though, she knew Moss was better prepared to scope out what was happening than she. If someone lurked about or if it a trap had been set, as she felt he suspected, she was too emotionally charged not to go off half-cocked.

She waited in the shadows for Moss to return. Freaked out a bit when she lost the sounds of his footsteps and, considering how tiny the cabin was, knew he'd gone into stalking mode. Her stomach twisted at not hearing the comforting sounds of him close by.

Finally, he called out that it was safe for her to join him. The cabin and yard were deserted.

So, where had they gone? Had Octavia and her nasty-ass swamp minions kidnapped them? Or had they seen the trouble coming and managed to elude them?

"I see no signs of a struggle, yet Octavia wouldn't have come and left with nothing," Moss stated, genuinely puzzled.

Beth knew he was right. Something was amiss. Octavia was far too vengeful to have come all this way only to leave empty-handed. She and Moss had just been in the other room, and Octavia would have sensed their presence. So why just leave? It didn't make a lick of sense.

Just then, the back door flew open, and Grace and Damien staggered in. Beth flew into her aunt's arms. Relief washed through her, calming her frayed nerves in an instant.

"What happened?" Beth asked still not having released Grace from her bear hug.

"I'm fine... *we're* fine. No reason to stress, honey. Damien sensed Octavia's presence just before she barreled out of the woods with those nasty little groupies of hers. We hid out in the swamps, and I sorta cast a wee little spell," Grace stated proudly. Her eyebrow cocked up as she shot a triumphant look at Damien, who grinned like the cat that ate the canary.

"A little spell? Uh oh. This should be good."

"Yes, wee—little. I couldn't touch her, but her lackeys were susceptible enough. She stormed off madder than a wet hen, no pun intended, her lackeys loudly in tow." Both she and Damien burst into laughter.

"And?" Beth pressed.

"They waddled closely behind, quacking the entire time," Damien finished for her.

"Quacking? As in *quack, quack* like a duck?" Beth snorted.

"Exactly like ducks. Very pissed off ducks with extremely loud quacks to boot," Grace added between gasps for breaths from laughing.

After they'd all managed to contain themselves, having had a much-needed break from all the stresses and emotions of the day, Beth remembered the spell she'd run across.

"Speaking of spells, I found one I think might be of use against Octavia. One that's sure to slam some of her own medicine down her throat." Good, she'd gained their undivided attention.

"Exactly which spell did you find?" Grace asked, sounding both curious and proud.

"Well it's similar to a redundancy spell but taken from chapter three, specializing in mirroring and erasing spells."

"Perfect. Utterly perfect." Grace beamed proudly. "I can't believe I'd forgotten about that old family recipe."

At the term *recipe*, both men bristled. Beth was sure neither would actually classify what had been done to them as a recipe, but after shooting each other speculative looks she understood they'd decided to stay mum about Grace's faux pas. So long as there was a way to stop Octavia's evil wrath, neither seemed to care who called it what.

The four worked through the night gathering the required ingredients for the potent spell, each growing quiet as the night drew on. Moss and Damien knew that if all went well, Octavia would no longer be in control of them.

But what of their own particular plights? What of changing back? Did they even still want to change back? All these years—no, centuries—of being at one with the swamps, could they give it up? More to the point, did they, deep down, even want to try? So much was riding on this spell, riding on Octavia's downfall.

Beth contemplated what Octavia's being out of the picture might mean for her. Yes, Moss cared for her. But would he still care when a virtual smorgasbord of gorgeous women was thrust at him? He'd been away from society for eons, and now, soon, he would be back among civilization. She could just imagine how women would react to him. All that predatory maleness wrapped up in a ripped package just ripe for the pickings.

Would he still think her beautiful compared to others of her gender? Or would she turn out to have simply been a choice of convenience, because there'd been no other to choose from? Her mind took in the image of her slightly bigger than average hips, breasts that weren't as high as they'd once been, and a stomach not as taut as years earlier. What would he think when he saw the beautiful, plastic people of today's world, with their silicone breasts in pert perfection and tummies tucked tighter than a military cot? Far more toned and defined than she, with their sickening, perfectly sculpted abs?

She cast a wayward glance toward Grace, noting her quiet state. What was rolling through Grace's mind? Was she worried as well about what would happen after Octavia was vanquished?

Secretly, Beth stared at Moss. He was silent, his posture stiff as he worked the task Grace had given him of finding assorted herbs out at the swamp's edge. He seemed methodical in his task, while lost in thought. As nervous as she was, the sight of his muscles bunching as he stretched and pulled native herbs from their roots had her nether regions quivering in excitement.

*

Moss gathered the requested items and acknowledged the butterflies swarming in his stomach. Freedom would soon be his, or so he hoped. There was no assurance the spell would revoke his or Damien's current states of being, but it was the closest hope either had ever had.

Would Beth still be attracted to him when he was a simple mortal again? Maybe he'd over thought the whole idea of setting her free because he wasn't human. Maybe the very danger that surrounded him had drawn her to him.

So damn much was at stake, for all of them.

He stood partially hidden by a cypress and watched Beth as she quietly exited the cabin. She went to stand at the porch banister as she scanned the area. Part of him longed to call her over to him. To tell her of his fears and pray she could put them to rest. Then there was the part of him that was too fearful to ask. The part that would take every last second they might have together and relish them.

He continued hiding behind the sanctity the cypress offered, watching in awe of her beauty. The way the moon made her blonde hair appear silvery as the gentle swamp winds played with it. The strands floating about so it appeared she had a halo. In truth, he didn't doubt her an angel sent from heaven above to rescue his dark soul.

She was as graceful as he imagined a celestial being would be, and as sweet as one too. Her heart was pure and wholesome as no other he'd met. Even more than his late wife's, whom he'd adored.

Moss watched her leave the porch and edge her way through the darkness down to the water's edge, a dangerous place to be in the evenings. Too many swamp predators came out to feed at this time.

Just before he reached her side, he saw her turn toward him, an unspoken fear passing between them. Moss sought to somehow reassure her—of what, he wasn't certain. He didn't like the thought of her fearing anything. What caused the moisture that glinted in her eyes? He stalked toward her, arms opening, and was comforted by the fact she turned, heading directly for him. Unfortunately, before she made it, before he could embrace her and assure himself that at least for now she was still his, Damien called out for both to return. Grace needed them.

He tried to smile, wanted to assure her no matter what the outcome with Octavia, Beth would forever hold his heart. While he wouldn't hold her to any promises previously made to him, she would always be his, whether she was with him, or free in her world.

*

Beth saw his tentative smile, as if he were unsure what to say. Was this the beginning or the end for them? Her heart felt as though it were about to break in two at not knowing for sure.

Wasn't that the saying? That not knowing something was sometimes the worse kind of hell? She could believe it. She'd been so close to asking. Close to throwing all the cards on the table and hoping for the best. Thankfully, Damien had saved her from possibly making an ass of herself. It wouldn't be the first time, and given her luck, it likely wouldn't have been the last.

Wordlessly, she took Moss's offered hand and they turned for the cabin. Just as they were about to enter, Moss grabbed her from behind, his hands firm and near bruising as he swung her around and laid one on her.

The kiss sucked all the air from her lungs, left her legs wobbly, Jell-O like, heating her blood as her heart pumped to catch up.

Her tongue gave back as it received, as did her hands as she groped the firm curve of his ass and pulled him into the cradle of her pelvis. Her clit rode the bulge behind his zipper, and she hissed at the delicious friction. His body seemed to shake under her hands as he pressed her firmly against the cabin's wooden door. For a split second, she thought to raise a leg over his hip, an offering, a pleading for more.

But there was much riding on what was to come.

Their futures.

Moss lifted his lips from hers, letting them linger them on her forehead before brushing gentle kisses above each eyelid.

"I will always love you," he vowed.

"And I you," she returned, knowing he could not promise

himself entirely to her until he at least got to see what the world had to offer. It wouldn't be right, no matter how badly it would hurt.

Grace opened the door as they stepped back to let them know everything was prepped for the ingredients they'd found. They were nearly ready for battle.

Chapter Twenty-Two

Thick, harsh smoke billowed from Octavia's cabin, no doubt from the strange herbs they'd discovered growing in baskets hanging from each corner of the porch. When they arrived, they'd found Octavia gone, but she'd left in a hurry as the stinky potions bubbling and steaming indicated. No one doubted they'd missed her by mere minutes. Why had she left? Had she been tipped off about their plan?

The first step of their plan was to obtain the *Book of Souls*. The book Damien had briefly seen but overheard much about. In this book were the names of all those Octavia had captured and turned. Beth hoped the bitch had made notes of what became of them. If a cure existed, it would be within the pages of this book. The cure for Moss and Damien was close, but not close enough. If they found it, Beth would make it her own personal goal to attempt to aid all the swamp creatures not born as such. Reflecting on what she'd learned of her aunt's betrothed, Beth supposed some might choose to remain as their animal or reptile counterparts.

Damien and Grace kept watchful eyes for Octavia's approach, while Beth and Moss scoured the place for the book. They grabbed any book that looked important. Or, in her opinion, creepy. Later, when they had more time, they would study the contents. Right now, though, they needed to search until they found the *Book of Souls* and the potential cure.

Step two of the plan was to destroy all magical things associated with Octavia. Her resources, strange ingredients, and every damn glass jar with funky shit inside. Essentially, they hoped to give her magic a severe handicap, and themselves an advantage. Step three, if they succeeded in accomplishing the first two, was to douse

Octavia in the brew Grace concocted. The potion should render her unable to perform any and all magic. Whether dark or light, she'd either be a powerless old woman, or there was the possibility that without her magic, she'd shrivel away to nothing.

Beth glanced out the window and caught her aunt studying Damien as he scanned the area. Both had been oddly quiet and distant since they'd arrived at Octavia's cabin. Had Damien been in love with the witch? Was he still? Grace seemed in awe of the warrior who carried his scars within. Something had tortured him emotionally.

Beth prayed his peculiar behavior was the product of the prospect of a cure and not some strange, twisted loyalty toward Octavia. He'd been with her for a very long time. Been a devoted and faithful companion who once thought himself in love with her. It would be strange if some sense of responsibility didn't linger. Why this thought only now came to mind Beth couldn't be sure, but suspected it had something to do with the way her aunt looked so longingly toward him. Beth caught an image in her aunt's mind of Damien embracing Octavia. The vision made Grace's stomach churn, then—poof—her link with Grace broke. Beth caught Damien stealing quick glances at Grace, a strange look on his face, as if he'd read her mind. Beth turned away from the window. She didn't have time to contemplate her own relationship, much less theirs.

Beth went to search for Moss when a strange feeling came over her. Strange, powerful and familiar. He'd gone into Octavia's bedchamber to pilfer around in the hopes of finding a secret compartment hiding the *Book of Souls*. She tried to call to him, but her vocal cords refused to cooperate. The sensation of ice pumping through her veins spread, freezing her to the core. It began at her throat and made its way rapidly procession to wrap its icy grip around her heart.

She couldn't call to Moss or anyone else. She remained frozen in place and in fear.

*

Moss turned the room inside out. He and Beth had already gone through every nook and cranny and come up empty handed. Short of the fact they'd at least destroyed much of Octavia's magical wares, this trip was a total bust. Yet he knew deep down the book was here. Its power called to him.

He stopped. Opened his senses and rescanned the room. Haunting memories of times past flooded back. Times best forgotten. Nights with Octavia in this very room, doing revolting things. Those dark memories rooted deep, caused horror to seep into his soul.

The first time he'd been with Octavia had been magical. He'd thought himself so beneath her. Though she'd used him as nothing more than a glorified slave, his heartbreak had driven him to consent to her every wish and twisted sexual fantasy. He'd thought her his savior—and now to learn she'd been the reason of the heartache… He'd followed her like the lamb to the slaughter.

She'd been beautiful. Exotic in every sense of the word. Long, lean, shapely legs…the type any man visualizes wrapped about his waist. Her long, dark hair cascaded about her like a midnight cloak. When she'd allowed him to undress her, he'd grown hard as a diamond. Her body was exquisite. Taut belly, firm breasts with mocha-tipped nipples. Mocha? He thought harder of that night. Of her appearance, trying to remember any flaw he'd overlooked. Shit, how had he not realized? He remembered now, quite clearly, the tiny, faint slivers of silver striping her belly.

Faint as they'd been, he'd seen them. Proof Octavia had a child. A child or, heaven forbid, children somewhere? Could he himself have fathered a child with her during one of their many trysts? And if his reasoning was on target, where were her children?

He turned to announce this possible bit of information when a floorboard creaked beneath his boot. Moss stepped back and forth over the area until a slight give in one of the boards, under the edge of the bed and against the far wall, revealed which one had creaked. Had he not gone so far, he'd never have found it.

Kneeling down, he ran his fingers about the board until he found the tiny rise separating the piece from the rest. With a gentle tug, the board sprang up. Hearing stones scraping together, he turned in time to see the fireplace jut from the wall an inch. The board itself was merely a trip lever for the hidden opening. He approached with apprehension and awe. In all the times he'd been in this room, he'd never known the secret passage existed.

"Impressive, Octavia. Impressive," he mumbled pulling the mantel back until there was enough space to allow his entry.

Though the passage was pitch black, his nocturnal eyes adjusted with ease until he made out a long, narrow passage leading to God only knew where.

He figured it best to get Beth before continuing and turned to yell for her when the wall behind him began moving until the doorway once again closed.

Now he had no choice but to continue along the corridor to wherever he ended up. Beth would discover his disappearance and seek Damien and Grace. One of the trio would realize what had happened. Would figure out he must have run across a passage such as this. Moss wondered if Damien had forgotten about it, or conveniently kept the information from them.

His unease about Damien skittered back. Had Damien truly gotten past his fixation with Octavia? The man had come forward and denounced his former lover, but his announcement at such, came while he'd been in front of Beth. Had it all been for show? Later, Grace had entered the picture and Moss knew beyond doubt the man wanted Grace. Damien's pheromones shot off the charts each time Grace came near him. Not to mention the times he'd caught Damien having to adjust himself. The man's raging hard-on was obviously quite uncomfortable. But his desire for Grace didn't prove his innocence.

Continuing down the dank, dusty, narrow corridor, he couldn't shake the distinct feeling of being watched, and his predatorily impulses peaked. He realized he was headed straight for a trap, but he had no way around it with nowhere to go except forward.

Silvery threads from the abundance of low-lying cobwebs wove themselves through his hair, and more than once the tickle of spider legs moved across his neck.

Fucking hate spiders.

A sulfuric scent burned his nose, clouding all other scents. He slowed his pace, crouching low, ready for an attack. Octavia was up to something. Only she would understand how strong his sense of smell was and know sulfur would mask his ability to smell potential danger.

Damn the old witch to hell.

He began to make out a glow in the distance, and other senses kicked in, screaming warnings. As the shadow forms became a tad more solid, he sprang back, but not quickly enough.

The three entities had him pinned and chained on the ancient floor before the last of his reptilian shift occurred.

*

"You've been rather lost in thought. Is everything okay?" Grace asked Damien, missing the warm warrior she'd grown fond of.

"No problems here," Damien bit out gruffly.

"You seemed a bit quiet, is all," Grace offered.

"Not quiet, observant."

She nodded, though she suspected his withdrawal stemmed from more than his being observant. Something had changed, but his one- and two-word answers proved he had absolutely no intentions of sharing what.

She followed the sudden jerk of his head, looking for whatever had caught his attention. Watched as he sniffed the air and seemed to bristle in response to what he scented. Nothing out of the ordinary came into sight, but she knew enough about Damien to believe his hackles didn't rise over nothing. They were no longer alone, and Damien was fully aware of this.

"What do you see?" she whispered.

"Nothing yet, but someone's watching us, and their scent is odd."

"Their scent?"

"Yes. You know I'm different. Where Moss has reptilian qualities, I have those of the armadillo. One of those differences is an acute sense of smell," he stated almost defensive, as if he thought her to be accusing him of something.

Oh, Grace thought, the *armor up, old chap* comment Moss had made back in the cave made sense now. "Didn't doubt you for a minute, but what should we do?"

"Go and warn the others." Again, his tone and demeanor seemed chilly.

Grace paused. He was off, and she needed to find out the reason for his sudden change. He might be a danger to them all right now. He may very well be their enemy.

"Go," he all but barked as his eyes took on an ominous appearance.

Deciding the best option was to go ahead and alert the others to the possible monkey—err—*armadillo* wrench in their plans, she took off to warn Beth. With her back to Damien, Grace couldn't help but feel like the hounds from hell rode her heels.

She went sailing through the front door, slamming the rickety thing with more force than intended and took a few deep, safe breaths. Her back against the door, she gave her very human eyes a minute to adjust to the dim interior.

Once they had, she was aghast at what was before her.

*

Livid he'd fallen for such an age-old trap, Moss struggled against the chains binding his arms. He'd been drawn up tight against the cave's wall, but struggling was useless short of making a clamor and cutting his wrists. He'd go nowhere any time soon. His shirt had been removed, as had his boots. He was thankful he'd at least been left with his pants, or what was left of them. After the near strip search, they were ripped in areas and sagging in others. What had pleased him even less had been where Octavia's eyes kept drifting. Her minions snickering as she lowered her gaze to the golden swatch of hair on his belly and lower still, until settling on his cock.

"You thought you'd just up and walk away, did you?" She ran her fingers, nails polished black, down his abdomen.

"That was the plan."

"Cocky boy. You thought what? I'd let you just whisk the slut off into the sunset and live happily ever after? Really, Moss, I'm surprised at you." Octavia all but purred as she fingered the outline of his flaccid member. If she anticipated getting a rise out of him, she'd be sorely disappointed.

"What I may or may not have thought is none of your damned concern. I will no longer be your lackey, Octavia. This ends now." Moss sneered.

"Well, someone ate their Wheaties this morning, didn't they?" She laughed. A true, mad, evil laugh, and nothing could have pissed him off more at the moment.

"Oh, did I bruise your tender male ego? Poor dear, I do tend to forget how sensitive you men can be."

Moss made out the three faint, shadowy shapes behind her in each corner of the room. Whoever or whatever they were, they stood motionless and cast no recognizable scent. That alone alarmed him more than any other shit she pulled.

"What evil things have you called upon now?" he asked with genuine curiosity.

"Whatever do you mean?" she asked, batting her eyelids in coy fashion.

"Playing stupid isn't becoming of you. Who are your newest lackeys? The ones hiding behind you?"

Octavia whirled around toward the closest shadow being. Once she'd reached him, she ran her palm over his abdomen, tracing around his entire middle until she reached his back. Then from behind him she toyed with his nipples, and no matter what she did, Moss noted the wavery figure never moved a muscle. Her hands continued to the bulge standing front and center, visible as darker than the rest of him, and stroked him with methodical intent.

Like one of the Queen's guards, the figure stood like a stone statue. She continued her seductive touches until she came to stand before him, and reached up and pulled his mouth to hers. Again, he knew the creature's mouth, as it was darker than the rest of him. The entity bent to her commands, his mouth locking with hers as a slight suction sound began. Only then did the entity's hands move of their own accord.

Moss continued watching in fascinated horror as Octavia seemed suddenly engulfed by this creature. Her body became more mist than flesh, as did the entity's. It was as if their bodies merged into one. Wisps of light and dark blended, circling like a tornado. The whirling grew more frenzied as small bursts of orange light shot from the center of the mass, growing until the dark became a deep shade of red.

So captured by the horror before him, he failed to notice another shadow sliding across the wall. Another witness to the mayhem about to erupt.

*

Beth stood in the center of the room, her pallor beyond white, her pulse all but gone.

"For the love of God, what in the hell happened, baby?" Grace didn't expect Beth to answer, as she suspected her niece was in the throes of a dark spell. The magic that encompassed the room was near suffocating as she smothered Beth with a healing spell. She needed to get Beth out of the cabin ASAP, before reversing the spell's poison became too dangerous to attempt. The longer some spells were present, the lower the likelihood anyone other than the one who cast it could remove it. She'd be damned if she'd lose Beth forever to a coma-like state until she literally withered to death.

Grace tried pulling her, but no matter how hard she tried, Beth remained anchored to the wooden floor. With each failed attempt, Grace grew more frantic. Beth's pulse became thready and weak as the spell continued to ravage her body. Damien feared a battle forthcoming outside, but she needed him, and now. She prayed whatever he'd sensed was long gone, or that he'd been wrong about it. Getting Beth out was now her top priority.

"Damien!" she screamed so loud her lungs burned. "Please, Damien. Beth's dying."

His silence worried her. Had he left? Had the change of heart she'd worried about caused him to switch sides? Grace hadn't long to worry—heavy, pounding footsteps shook the cabin floors as Damien barreled through the door.

"Outside." Tears loomed in the corners of her eyes. "We have to get her outside this cabin if we've any hope of saving her." As much as she wanted to break at the prospect of losing Beth, she wouldn't. She *couldn't*. She refused to let her niece down.

Damien omitted a few grunts and huffs but managed to break Beth free from the magical hold. He slung her over his shoulder and all but lunged for the door.

Once outside the magical coffin Octavia called a cabin, Grace began her work. After a good length of time, Beth's color flooded

Swamp Magic

back into her cheeks, then her body. Moments after, Beth sat up ramrod straight and slung obscenities at the coward who refused to fight face-to-face.

"Shush, now. You'll get yours, but right now we need to exercise patience and caution," Grace urged.

"Where the hell was Moss when you got attacked?" Damien seethed.

She opened her mouth to answer, but realized she hadn't a clue. The spell cast upon her had been silent, but wouldn't he have least heard the chaos of her being hauled outside? Of Grace screaming for Damien? Even in her induced coma state, she'd heard Grace's scream. She hadn't been able to respond, but she'd been conscious of everything throughout the event. She started toward the cabin but a vise-like grip wrapped around her forearm, jerking her to a stop.

"What?" she squawked.

"You almost died and you're going back in? I don't think so. You two stay out here. I'll go search the place," Damien told her.

"Actually, that's not a bright idea either," Grace protested. "You aren't immune to Octavia's craft, either. We'll go together. After the invisible assault on Beth, I think staying together is our best option right now."

"Agreed," both Beth and Damien answered simultaneously.

After a thorough search turned up an empty cabin, Beth's stomach began to roll.

"So where the hell did he go?" Damien asked to neither in particular.

"Damn good question if you ask me," Grace replied, knowing Beth had been concerned about Damien's loyalties and now feared she'd worried about the wrong man.

"He went into Octavia's room and I guess vanished. Poof—gone." Beth all but bit her tongue to keep from adding her fear she'd been played after all. Maybe he'd had a change of heart. Moss had been with Octavia a long time. Had she threatened him? Either way, shit didn't add up. The hostility in his voice each time he spoke Octavia's name left her leaning toward a threat, but he had acted off back at the cabin earlier that day. When he'd stormed off claiming to need some quiet time. What if that had been a ruse and he'd gone off to forewarn Octavia?

She and Grace watched as Damien slowly circled the room, rather like an Indian tracking something. His posture was stiff and guarded, on high alert.

"Damien, what do you detect?" Curious, Grace began following his movements. He seemed to be testing the floorboards.

"I believe there to be a hidden passage. She's too paranoid to ever leave herself caged in. She would have an escape route."

"You bet she would. Half the damn swamp probably wants to make kibble out of her. But…"

Both turned when Beth trailed off, the elephant in the room heavy and suffocating. Did Moss use the possible escape willingly or unwillingly? The situation was grave for both men, as their lives hung in the balance from the battle's outcome.

"There's far too much on the table to speculative. Let's just find this hidden route, kill the old bitch, find Moss, and get our answers." Grace picked up her pace, tapping on walls and floors as she tried to listen for any hollow sound. The others followed suit until finally Damien stumbled upon the loose board.

"Well, I'll be damned," Grace sputtered, peering into the blackened passageway.

"I'm sure she's booby-trapped it in anticipation of intruders." Damien advised as he investigated the surrounding area.

"I'm prepared." Again stunning everyone, Grace began to glow. Not a full-on glow, but rather an effervescent sparkle. "What?"

"Nothing," Beth and Damien answered in unison.

Oh, yeah, she and Grace were long overdue for a serious powwow. Apparently her family had far more than a few skeletons skulking about.

Though this new disclosure was great timing, Beth snatched the heavy brass candlestick off the mantel as they entered. Damien had his armor and superior strength, her aunt had who-knew-what powers, and Beth had a candlestick.

Wow, odd duck out sucks ass.

*

Moss awoke with his head about to burst like a melon and the vague memory of Octavia's odd merging with the unknown entity. He still wasn't sure where he was. This cave was new to him, and he was familiar with almost every inch of the swamp.

"So you're awake again."

The male voice was unfamiliar. He squinted to make out the hazy form lingering in the shadows.

"Who are you?" he croaked, fighting back the bile rising from the excruciating pain radiating through his head.

"It isn't so much who I am as what I am. But you have a right to be curious, though I should remind you, curiosity killed the cat."

"Good thing I'm not a pussy then." He took in the guy's weaselly appearance. Dark greasy hair, no more than about five-foot nine, and soaking wet he couldn't have weighed more than a hundred and fifty pounds.

"Brave, are we?" the man said.

"Tired of playing charades. So who—excuse me, *what*—are you?"

"Powerful, deadly, and Octavia's true heir. I'm tired of my mother's uh…dalliances. It's gone from embarrassing to a nuisance encroaching on dangerous to, ah, certain friends."

"Is your mother aware you still play with imaginary friends?"

His quip earned him the bite of knuckles. On a scale of hard knocks it barely ranked, but coupled with his raging headache it nearly rendered him unconscious.

"Head hurt?"

"Not from that love tap." Yeah, another strike, but the attacks were causing his adrenaline to rise, aiding in clearing his mind from whatever drug they'd slipped him. His reptile side slithered to the surface and for the first real time he could recall, he embraced this other side. Encouraged it forth.

"So clearly you've got some mommy issues. What? She wasn't soothing enough? Loving enough? No? How could she be when she was too busy out spreading her love with all of us? Must have been a real bitch growing up. Literally."

Bam—more knuckles.

"So brave now, but with mother dearest out of the way, I wonder how long you continue."

Moss's threat was empty. The hate between Octavia and son simmered, ready to boil over, fierce enough the man's judgment was seriously off kilter, which suited Moss fine. It would be easier to take the ass out. Had the son taken out his mother first, then gone after each of her creations one at a time, he might have succeeded. Instead, he gathered her creatures out of spite—not an optimal situation. What this whiny-ass brat didn't realize was that although he and Damien had no issues with his offing mommy, there'd no doubt be creatures that would. Who would be ready to fight to the death for her.

"Never realized the boy she spoke of would turn out to be as whiny as she claimed," Moss prodded.

"Nice try, but my mother would have never admitted to having a son."

"Wrong. She did, after a good romping. I'd asked about children, noticing those wicked little scars on her stomach. She explained her hell-spawn created them. I'm not sure which she claimed more disgust over. The stretchmarks, or you. Speaking of, other than as 'her biggest regret' she never mentioned your name. Feel free not to tell me. I can always use one of the other more colorful names she called you. Regret, weakling…"

Crack.

"You will address me as master, because that's what I'll be as soon I take charge. Her fondness for men is to be her downfall. She was far too soft on you all, but that is about to change. You will be in my control and will do my bidding."

"Oh, I get it now. Baby boy can't get his own homeboy to play with, so you need to steal your mother's. Perfectly clear now."

Whack.

Though the imbecile's strikes lacked any serious strength, they did get on his nerves.

*

With Damien leading and Grace at her rear, Beth had a false sense of security. She wisely ignored that sense, having learned the hard way a time or two. Octavia would anticipate their arrival, but the uncertainty about Moss unsettled her more than what hid in the dark. He'd grieved all those years over the loss of his wife and the children; of this, she was positive. Had he decided to confront Octavia on his own? Did he doubt her word that Octavia was behind it all?

"Look out!"

The alarm from Damien came not a moment too soon. They'd just rounded a bend in the passageway when something from above attacked Damien. Beth made a move to assist him, but Grace knocked her back against the wall. Another shadowy creature came sailing down from above, this one setting its sights on Grace. With both Grace and Damien fighting unknown assailants, that left Beth and her brass candlestick to fend off the dark shadow slithering her way. She could scarcely make out what it was, but the darker shade on the ceiling was most certainly moving toward her.

Beth readied her weapon and stood her ground, wishing she knew how the others fared. She didn't dare take her eyes off the inky movement on the ceiling, though, and prayed both held their own. The air around her grew thick and moist though oddly chilled. She forced her mind to a calm place, ignoring her now-jittery nerves, and swung just as the thing launched itself at her. Remarkably, the candlestick sailed right through whatever it was, as if it were made of smoke not substance.

Damn it.

A sudden, searing pain struck her side as the dark mass swirled about her. She heard shouts but not what they screamed, just the distinct sounds of stress. Panic set in at the sound of Grace in distress and Damien's battle growls, but she didn't dare take the time to even look, not until she knew where the inkblot from hell had gone. Her heart pounded and blood whooshed through her ears as terror struck her. The mass seemed to be taunting her, provoking her to sheer madness as she swung wildly about.

From deep within the madness something snapped. A peaceful calm swept through her, leaving in its path a powerful feeling. Everything around her appeared outlined in a bright blue. She pulled energy from the light, absorbed as much of it as she could. Centered her entire being on the power it contained. Without forethought, she blasted the mass as well as the entire passageway with a blinding white light that shot from her hands.

*

Moss felt the blast, as did the butthead. The walls shook and crumbled around them as small pebbles shook loose from the cave's ceiling. Dynamite? Who the hell would be blasting in an unsecured cave system?

"Marcus, Gregor, go investigate."

Two shadows lifted themselves from the cave's wall and took on human form. He wasn't sure if they were ghost, zombie, or other. They were more mist than flesh and were like nothing he'd ever seen.

"Impressive, aren't they?" Though he refused to ask, Moss hoped Octavia's son would choose to explain. "There were created much like you were. I, however, enhanced their abilities by creating them as more of a swamp gas than actual creature. Essentially, I've created creatures with few known foes. They have no real enemies, natural or otherwise, to speak of."

Moss saw a strange orb form, stopping to hover behind Demetrius. Moments later it turned into a more misty like substance before taking a decidedly, human shape. Moss didn't look away from Demetrius, instead he watched from his peripheral vision. He suspected Octavia had arrived and was curious as to what Mommy Dearest would think about her darling son's deceitful plans.

"Abominations are what they are."

"Mother, how kind of you to join us." Demetrius kept his tone cool, but Moss caught his startled look before schooling his expression and facing his Mother.

"Demetrius, I demand to know what you have done this instant."

So, Demetrius, was it? Good to know.

"Mother, you've outlived your usefulness, and the others have grown impatient with your dalliances."

"Have they? And you, my own son, have chosen to side with them?"

"I understand their points clearly and agree. You have been nothing but a disgrace to our society. You are a whore, and your time has passed. I have requested your life be spared on the condition that you vacate the area and cease any and all magic."

"How thoughtful of you, but I believe you underestimate my attentions where you are concerned. I may have reluctantly carried you, but you have been nothing but a reminder of a lapse in judgment."

Moss could sense the air changing around them. The molecules became charged, and though he had nowhere to go, he braced for the attack. Marcus and Gregor still stood frozen in place. Neither had moved an inch, though Demetrius had issued the command to investigate.

Demetrius began to shimmer, alternating between solid form and mist. Octavia, too, began flickering as the air grew thicker by the moment.

Sparks seem to radiate from both as their forms wavered in and out. The storm was coming, and Moss had no way to shelter from it. He thanked the heavens Beth and the others were safely away from the impending battle.

A scraping drew his attention to the trap door he'd been dragged through, and Moss was horrified when the wall opened to reveal Damien carrying Beth's still form through the door.

"Stay back! Things are about to get bad," Moss roared.

Damien quickly shielded his charge from the blast of the two powerful entities colliding.

*

"Damn it, put me down. I may not know exactly what I did, but I know it was bad-assed. It just startled me for a moment." Beth twisted and wiggled until finally Damien lost his grip and set her back on her feet. Grace dashed through next, whirling her around until they were face to face.

"Yes, there is much to explain, and I swear I will later, but for now, know you too are quite powerful, and if you can pull from your inner magic again, do so now."

"I would if I understood what I did in the first place."

"You pulled from within and found your hibernating magic. It's always been there, lying dormant, but you never needed it enough for it to fully awaken."

She heard Grace's words, but couldn't concentrate after she took in Moss's bloody form across the room. Shackled to the wall, he bore wounds indicating he'd borne the brunt of either Octavia's or her opponent's rage. His shoulder had a wide gash that clearly needed stitches, and two of his fingers were just dangling, broken.

Breaking from Grace's hold, Beth dashed through the eruptions of clashing magic. Fire, falling rocks, and whatever the hell the misty shit was, sprang all around creating a freakish war zone. Beth raced oblivious of the dangers until she reached Moss's side.

"Damn you, woman, do you realize what danger you just put yourself in?" Moss bellowed.

"Pfft. You damn well better be glad you're hurt, or else that woman crack would land you another hurting."

At the sounds of even more falling debris, Beth risked a glance over her shoulder and saw Damien and Grace battling the duo before them. It appeared the former enemies had decided to unite, even if for just the moment.

"Okay, I got Octavia but who the hell is he?" Beth pointed to the man now standing at Octavia's right. A puny man, thin yet by all accounts muscular as he took on Damien. His slick, dark hair was laced with threads of silver, and had she not seen his squinty, beady eyes, might have described him as distinguished. But that pinched face of his left her with the lasting impression of a rodent.

"He is Demetrius, Octavia's son." As if he could read her thoughts, Moss growled low in his throat. "Free me so that I may join in the battle."

"Remember, Moss, we haven't found the book with the spells to undo the curse, so you cannot kill Octavia," she reminded him as she sought the key to release the shackles.

"Move over a bit," Grace yelled above the melee.

Beth turned to question but saw her aunt raise her hands in their direction and quickly moved aside as a white light whizzed past.

Sure as shit, Moss's bindings fell open.

Before Beth could utter another word, Moss stormed into the middle of the fight, which now consisted of Damien, Demetrius, and the two misty creatures. That left Beth and Grace with Octavia, which suited her just fine. The bitch was about to learn what bad was.

Chapter Twenty-Three

"Well, well. We meet again."

"Yes we do, but it will be the last time, I promise you that," Grace seethed at her rival.

"Only time will tell. You're not still pissed over that poor pitiful sap you called a fiancé, are you? I thought we settled that back at Damien's? I did you a favor, remember?"

The taunt had been thrown, but thankfully Beth noted the absence of a counterstrike from her aunt. Not this time. Beth smiled, wondering if the sudden change had anything to do with the sexy hulk of a man currently straining to check on her.

Damien was busy fending off the misty things but continued to cast glances their way, making sure Grace remained safe and holding her own. Who knew they'd both find handsome, eligible men out in the swamps?

"He isn't yours, young one, and he never will be." Octavia spat through gritted teeth.

Beth whipped her head around at Octavia's statement and took glee that the other woman carried an uncertainty about her now. She was unnerved by their presence and united powers. Hopefully they could keep her that way long enough to extract the cure for Moss and Damien and any other victims she'd left out in the swamp.

"You haven't seen him trying to off me, now, have you?"

Octavia's eyes shimmered an ominous, unnatural red. Beth loved seeing Octavia bristle as her barb about Moss landed. The real battle was about to begin. Closing her eyes to the chaos around, she rooted within until she found the place the power resided. She drew deep as Grace had instructed and called upon the magic once more.

When she opened her eyes, she was vaguely aware of their glow, a shimmery blue. Bright, blinding blue, and of Octavia's sudden wariness.

Octavia raised an arm and threw out an arc of red light, blasting both Beth and Grace clear across the room. Before they could recover, another blazing bolt blasted from Octavia's palm, and they nearly didn't scramble fast enough. One after another, these strange arcs of lightning came, and Beth sensed her aunt's growing exhaustion. She'd been tossing up fields, blocking as many of the arcs as she was able, and the power she expelled was taking its toll. Out of the corner of her eye, Beth saw Moss and Damien get the upper hand, but neither was in a position to help.

She squared off with the bitch and found the energies she'd called on waiting, building, *ready.*

Again the odd, out-of-body-like sensation zipped through her, making her feel as though she were witnessing things through someone else's eyes. Only, unlike before, she felt the unmistakable power centering in her palms. Knew the power there awaited her command. Then she unleashed it. The power flew unchecked, and she pondered the idea of releasing such magic when she knew nothing about it. By then it was too late.

The power hit Octavia dead on, but also blew through the chamber. Only by a miracle did it not cause a cave-in.

When the dust and debris settled, Octavia lay dead on the floor and only Damien, Moss, and Grace remained.

The trio stared open-mouthed at Beth, and then everything around her spun. Darkness engulfed her.

*

When she came to, she was lying in her aunt's bed with a cool washrag across her forehead. "What happened?" She croaked as Grace's blurry face came into better view.

"We won the battle," Grace answered with sheer pride in her expression.

"So Octavia and her crew are gone?"

"Unfortunately, Demetrius—her son—and his minions vanished, and we aren't sure what happened to them. He was in the process of threatening Grace when the blast occurred," Damien muttered, entering the room, obviously having overheard their conversation. Beth could tell he was clearly concerned about Demetrius and his lackey's vanishing act.

"What do you mean he was threatening Grace?"

"Well, apparently Demetrius took a shine to Grace and was proceeding to tell me his quite graphic plans for her. I was setting him straight when I was interrupted."

Beth caught a private glance between Damien and Grace—a flash of something protective from Damien and wistful from Grace. Though Beth would like to drill her aunt about what was happening between her and Damien, she decided it was more important to remember what had transpired before she'd passed out. To her horror, the image of Octavia's bloody, lifeless body, sprawled in an unnatural angle gurgled to memory.

"Oh, my God. I killed her before we got the reversal spell." Beth sat up, pulling her knees to her chest. The men must hate her. She'd blown their chance at returning to a normal life. After warning Moss not to kill her, she had. Oh, yeah, he would hate her. How could she have been so reckless? Her insides turned and tears burned, threatening to spill as she realized any future with her beloved Bog Man had died when Octavia had. Worse, though, she'd destroyed his future.

"Well, when one's magic first comes to them, the power can be a bit unpredictable. Unstable, even. But in time and with practice, you will learn to harness the energy."

"I ruined two lives and God only knows how many others by using it. I think it's best if we forget I even found my magic."

"What did you ruin?" a deep voice asked.

Grace rose after giving her niece a peck on the cheek and winked at Moss as she and Damien passed him on their way out. Beth and Moss needed to talk privately.

"Yours, Damien's and countless others. Oh, Moss, I'm so damn sorry. I didn't mean to kill her. She lashed out so quickly, and Grace was growing so weary from blocking and I just…just… unleashed without thinking." It all came out as one long-winded ramble, and Moss chuckled, surprising her. He hadn't cursed her or run from the room. Actually, he didn't even appear cross with her.

"Quit beating yourself up. You did what you had to do, and I couldn't be more proud."

"But I lost your chance at becoming human again," she reminded him, though she really didn't want to.

"Maybe, maybe not. Who knows? The book may turn up eventually. More important to me than any cure is you."

She stared at him, speechless.

"Your safety and happiness mean more to me than any possible cure. Why do you think I left you that night?"

"I kinda thought because I was a one-night stand."

He sat on the edge of the bed and pulled her into his arms. "Far from it. I found everything I ever wanted in life when I found you. I feared keeping you with me here in the swamp would stifle that fiery spirit of yours. I couldn't ask that of you. I love you too much for that, Beth."

"Oh, hell, no. You better not think you're going anywhere without me, buddy. You just dropped the L word, and it's on now."

*

Moss had hoped Beth would accept him as he was and would remain with him, but he hadn't banked on it. Now, the little vixen crawled into his lap and aggressively turned his head for a kiss.

Maybe his little swamp flower had enough thorns to be happy in the swamps, or maybe she didn't. But there was only one way they'd find out, he thought, scooping her into his arms as they headed for his cabin.

Yeah, the path to discovery would be a bit bumpy, but filled with unimaginably wicked nights.

About the Author

Author Bobbi Romans born and raised in the suburbs of D.C, now resides in the south with Prince Charming and her overly large, nutty family. Currently, Bobbi is hiding from her loud family in a closet as she taps away the next installment in the Swamp Magic series, *Swamp Magic—Under the Full Moon*. The story of Grace and her Armadillo shifter, Damien.

Look for updates and contests from Bobbi at her website *www.bobbiromans.com* or on Facebook *www.facebook.com/pages/Bobbi-Romans* or on Twitter here: *https://twitter.com/BobbiRomans*

In the mood for more Crimson Romance? Check out *Forever and Ever, Amen* by Liv Rancourt at *CrimsonRomance.com*.

Made in the USA
Lexington, KY
13 October 2013